GW00738468

Litro Magazine is the UK's largest read free short stories and creative arts magazine, in print and online. Litro's ethos is finding new ways of looking at the world through stories. Traditionally Litro focused on short fiction, armed with a mission to discover new and emerging writers, giving them a platform to be read alongside stalwarts of the literary scene. Publishing debut writers for 10 years now, Litro has launched the careers of many first time writers such as; Sarah Butler, Stuart Evers, Richard House (ManBooker longlisted), Nikesh Shukla, and many more. Now Litro has added more strings to its bow developing a fully fledged online platform a place for readers, writers and the broader creative community to discuss various aspects of literature, arts and culture through features, reviews, non-themed fiction, interviews, columns.

"Well, Litro was the start of a run of good things for me. Since that fateful issue in 2009, I've had a novel published and nominated for a few awards, called Coconut Unlimited. I co-wrote an ebook about the urban youth with Kieran Yates called Generation Vexed. I also went on to write a pilot for Channel 4's Comedy Lab series called Kabadasses."
Nikesh Shukla

We hope that you will engage with the stories set within the pages of this anthology, and who knows they may inspire to tell your own. As long as you have a good story, we want to hear it. You can join the Litro community by visiting us at www.litro.co.uk

Hearing
Voices

The Litro Anthology
of
New Fiction

PUBLISHED BY LITRO MAGAZINE in association with
KINGSTON UNIVERSITY PRESS

Litro Magazine, 1-15 Cremer Street, Studio 21.3, London
E2 8HD, England

Kingston University, Penrhyn Road, Kingston upon Thames
KT1 2EE, England

ISBN : 978-1-899999-74-3

Production team:

Naomi Peel
Danny Lyle
Katie Hatcher
Laura Bryars
Ben Duncan

Cover Design:

Elizabeth Mims
Ditte Loekkegaard

Introduction

There's something magical about the way stories can transport us. Whether we're curled up at home on the sofa or squeezed between strangers on the tube, all it takes is a turn of the page – or, in this technological age, a swipe of the screen – to open a portal to a different time, a different place, or even the inside of someone's head. The migration of film and TV to handheld devices hasn't altered the unique spell of the written word. There's no better way to escape the world around you than burying yourself in a book.

Litro has always taken a global view of the literary landscape, publishing writers from across Britain and far, far beyond its shores. *Hearing Voices* collects some of the best writing to have passed through the pages of the magazine during the ten years of its existence, and some of the most exciting authors to have graced its pages, as well as five new writers selected by Kingston Writing School. There are stories here from authors on both sides of the Atlantic, spanning locations as far apart as Ithaca and Nairobi – and even the surface of the moon. What connects them is the strength of their voices, and the vibrant originality of their storytelling.

The collection opens in globetrotting style, with stories that display the international scope of Litro. Anthony Doerr is already a literary star in the US – his latest novel, *All The Light We Cannot See* (2014), was an international bestseller and a finalist for the 2014 National Book Award. It's little wonder that his opening story, 'Trees', is so finely nuanced, and so moving. Lucie Whitehouse is British by birth and education, but currently lives in New York, where her story, 'Early', takes place. Chloe Aridjis's story 'Pigeon' uses London as its setting, but in its tradition – and its backdrop – its debt is to Aridjis' Mexican heritage. Looking further afield, Nikesh Shukla hits the road in Nairobi with 'The Circus Safari and Other Marvels', while Nigerian-Flemish writer Chika Unigwe's 'Saving Agu's Wife' tells a unique and touching tale of a Nigerian refugee in Belgium. Then there's Jeremy Tiang's Germanic 'Schwellenangst', and ''Til God', a tale of youthful dissent and rebellion set in Cyprus by Polis Loizou. Loizou based the story on a real incident from his youth – we can only hope that wasn't why he decided to relocate to London.

There are also tales set closer to home. Barry McKinley's 'Job' examines a specific moment in British history through a drug-induced haze, while Laura McKenna's 'Cable' picks at the seams of a sibling relationship against a very Irish backdrop. Our closing story, 'Doted' by Jenn Ashworth, takes Northern England as its setting, although its tradition stretches back as far as Shakespeare, reimagining King Lear in a contemporary setting. Historian Kate Williams also stays firmly rooted in Britain's past, with her sinister look at the madness of witchcraft trials in 'The Weakness of Hearts' – her first attempt at a short story, published in the pages of Litro. Joanna Walsh, meanwhile, takes a sideways glance at what it means to be British in 'The Story of our Nation'. You'll never see the English hedgerows in quite the same way again.

A writer's imagination is not confined by the opportunities presented by the real world, however. It also allows for leaps of the imagination. Ian Sales has an impressive track record as a science fiction author, but his story here – 'The Spaceman and the Moon Girl' - is grounded in a specific moment in history, like a reworking of Mad Men for the Space Race era. AMC should sit up and take notice. 'The Girl with the Sausage Dog' by Alexander Knights was longlisted for the Bath Short Story Award, and it's easy to see why: in its combination of hi-tech gadgetry and untraditional romance it sounds like a voice for the future. The same can be said of Tara Isabella Burton's 'Ivan Returns to Ithaca', a story laced with grit and fantasy in equal measure. We're confident that both will be writers to watch in years to come. Another emerging talent, Iain Robinson, imagines a world in turmoil, and the lengths a parent would go to in an era of post-apocalyptic barbarism, in 'Kids Come Looking. Kids Come Back.'

Other writers choose to explore psychological landscapes, every bit as strange and unique as their geographical counterparts. 'A Religious Experience' by Charlie Hill reveals a darker, more serious side to his writing than his current satirical novel, *Books*; F.C. Malby's 'Clipboards and White' is equally unsettling, as it opens the door on mental illness. In 'Prey', Michelle Wright looks at the aftermath of sexual assault with a bold and unflinching gaze: this is one of those stories that stays with you long after you have finished reading it. Seth Clabough feels shockingly contemporary in 'To Become Immortal', a story propelled as much by its style as its narrative, while Reece Choules' 'Seen and Not Seen' combines the best of both: a dynamic, tragic story told in a unique and compelling voice.

Finally, there are those who work their way under the skin of their characters, young and old. Samuel Wright, Howard Cunnell and Trine V. Ipsen have all chosen to work with young narrators, each handling in different ways the palate of innocence and disaffection these provide. 'Old', '13' and 'Postcards from Paradise' are very different stories, but all three show that childish eyes often see more than we imagine. There's even space for lighter interludes, with Alan McCormick's witty – but slightly disturbing – look at celebrity stalkers, 'Message to You', and Sean Beaudoin's great American rock opera, 'Steve-O in Seven Movements'. Both coax a wry smile with their satirical glance at celebrity culture.

Hearing Voices showcases the wide range of literary talent that has passed through Litro's pages, from emerging young writers to established stars with several books to their name. We're justifiably proud of the number of new Litro writers who have gone on to successful careers as published novelists. For this reason we've chosen to open the collection with a poem by Benjamin Zephaniah, originally published by Litro in 2008. The poem, 'What If', neatly encompasses the spirit of equality and diversity that Litro has always taken as its cornerstone, and which underpins this anthology. Sometimes all a new writer needs is a box to stand on, and a megaphone to talk to the world. Hopefully Litro will help these voices be heard for many years to come.

Eric Akoto and Dan Coxon
Litro Magazine Editors

What If

Benjamin Zephaniah

If you can keep your money when governments about you
Are losing theirs and blaming it on you,
If you can trust your neighbour when they trust not you
And they be very nosy too;
If you can await the warm delights of summer
Then summer comes and goes with the sun not seen,
And pay so much for drinking water
Knowing that the water is unclean.

If you seek peace in times of war creation,
And you can see that oil merchants are to blame,
If you can meet a pimp or politician,
And treat those two imposters just the same;
If you cannot bear dis-united nations
And you this dis new world order is a trick,
If you've ever tried to build good race relations,
And watch bad policing mess your work up quick.

If you can make one heap of all your savings
And risk buying a small house and a plot,
Then sit back and watch the economy inflating
Then have to deal with the negative equity you've got;
If you struggle on when there is nothing in you,
Except the knowledge that justice cannot be wrong.
If you can speak the truth to common people
Or walk with Kings and Queens and live no lie,
If you can see how power can be evil
And know that every censor is a spy;
If you can fill an unforgiving lifetime
With years of working hard to make ends meet,
You may not be wealthy but I am sure you will find
That you can hold your head high as you walk the streets.

Trees

Anthony Doerr

He stops at the supply room window, a floor-to-ceiling sheet of glass, double-paned, six feet wide. The best window in the entire building. Third story, forty feet up. He has been in here maybe three thousand times and hasn't noticed this window once. Maybe they've stripped it of blinds, or hauled some obscuring shelf away.

The view looks into the heart of the grand old tree which stands just behind the Company's entrance sign. He thinks it is an oak but it might be something else. A maple? He has that dry, wooden film in his mouth that he always gets in the afternoons at work: something close to the smell of the Company cafeteria an hour after lunch, three or four engineers at long tables staring into their baked chicken.

They make memory here. Semiconductors. Every hour is a tribulation.

In the supply room, forty feet up, the branches of the tree are thin, forking into glossy twigs, and ornamented with seeds. Waving yellow ropes of light slip down through the boughs, and the leaves look to him like small hands, ten thousand of them, each moving of its own inclination, but all of them moving somehow in concert, showing their palms to the sun.

He intended to retrieve a box of purchase order blanks. Instead some thin and final membrane inside him gives way and he picks his way through the cubicles, not even pausing when Fred Simpson tries to show him a piece of paper, and goes down the fire exit and stands beneath the tree, oak or maple.

The bark presents a storm of texture – canyons and ridges and caves. A column of big black ants ascends the trunk, wallowing in its grooves.

A half hour later he is in the public library in his khakis and knit tie, with his plastic name badge still around his neck, paging through a book called *Trees*. Paulownia. Catalpa. The glory of cherries. Spruce. Stone pine. Maple. There it is: Norway maple. He has to apply for the library card.

At home his wife says, "You're home early," and he says, "Yes I am." He fumbles through boxes in the basement. There is a 35-millimeter Nikon FG-20 buried in here somewhere, beneath football jerseys and an antler chandelier she'd made him take down.

All through dinner she asks questions about work. To pacify her, he says he has managed to collect some overdue funds from Hitachi, one of the "majors." This is an outright lie. The tree book sits on the hall table, waiting.

The house is old but new to them. They have moved to it to escape the memories, but the memories wander the halls after them, relentless, unabating: night-time feedings, the gurgling he would make in his crib, the sour, powdery smell of his formula.

He didn't last, their son. Gave up after ten months, called it quits. They'd used the Nikon on him plenty.

In bed he studies cracks in the ceiling paint and dreams dreams: he'll make a book, he'll travel the world, he'll photograph trees, the Magic hawthorn, the famous pears of Bethesda. An acacia in Africa. A lenga in patagonia. A tree book, pages of trees.

In the morning he drives to three drugstores before he finds film. Then he takes the Toyota right past the main entrance of the Company, past the Norway maple, past the sixty-two new emails waiting for him on his desktop computer, and drives into the hills to where the Company has cut swaths to accommodate incoming power lines.

He hikes in the steep grass in his cross-trainers, the camera banging his ribs. Thrushes sing like little waterfalls in the branches. There are hedge maples up there, and what might be a paperbark maple. Some others: a tulip tree, a cottonwood; he isn't entirely sure.

He packs a roll of film into the Nikon and trains the viewfinder up, where the smallest branches break the sky.

F-stop, film speed, focus. Exposure.

Again he has the feeling that the leaves are hands, palms-up. Entreating. Imploring. Far below him he can see the gravelled roof of the nanoFab building, and the back wall on Administration, twin columns of black windows. Somewhere behind those windows Steve Keating is walking to the 10am Collections Meeting and Katie the intern is pushing buttons on the copier and Harriet Stover is pausing in a hallway, thumbing a message into her phone.

By 10:30am he has exposed four rolls. He brings it to Albertson's One Hour, the last developer in the city, and sits waiting while the machines whirr and click and a mom runs six neon green bottles of soda through a self-service scanner.

The pictures are lousy. A bunch of branches, not all of them in focus. Nothing like he had hoped. Nothing to suggest the thrushes, the leaves, the way the trees slowly gathered their shadows beneath them like trembling networks of darkness.

But. Success does not come overnight.

For a week of dinners he is able to maintain the lie. "They need me to go out of town next week."

"No, I don't know where the dust on the car came from."

"No, I don't know why Harriet Stover called three times."

But on Monday he returns from a morning of shooting birches above a farm (two dogs snapping at him and he'd stumbled into a bog) to find her at the table furious. "You went today," he guesses. "To the office."

"An affair," she says.

"Trees."

"I don't get it."

"What's to get? I'm going to Salt Lake tomorrow. Not for work. Not for anything. For the aspens."

She glares at the surface of the table and – slowly, awfully – punches holes in her sandwich with an index finger. She says, "This is about Oliver."

"Yes. No. Maybe." He sighs. In the months after the death of their son, he has become a virtuoso sigher. Sighs like transcontinental airliners, sighs like great billboards, sighs like the wake of a ship in the ocean.

This particular one is a bridge, cantilevered for a moment into the space between them, then collapsing.

The lobes of her ears tremble. "And the pay cheque?"

"Really? The paycheck?"

"Nine years and you up and quit? Without even discussing it?"

"There was this window. A Norway maple."

"This is not what people do."

"I'm trying," he says. "I'm working on it."

That night he lies on the sofa with the camera balanced on his gut. She is at Kristie's. Maybe Megan's. A car passes and the arcs of its headlights sweep across the ceiling, carrying the shadows of leaves. The wind moans in the chimney. He feels it again: the urge to run. He yanks open windows and lets his heart thud against the darkness. According to 'Trees,' there are huge groves of aspens in Utah in which each tree is a clone of every other, all of them rising from the same ultra-complicated root system, so many roots interlaced and webbed through the soil that the trees function as a single, hundred-acre organism. One plant, one hundred acres, six million kilograms. Eighty-thousand years old.

In mid-September, the book says, the leaves of these groves all lose their chlorophyll at once, flaring yellow and orange and sometimes a little red, streaks of flames on all the mountains. How can he have lived forty-four years and not seen this?

Out there Company trucks are being loaded with pallet after pallet of high-density memory. Out there clouds are scudding over the city: not a single one the same as any other. The biggest boat ever built, he thinks, was a crumb on the great blue sea. A line from a children's book, one of Oliver's.

On the flight to Salt Lake he trades for a window seat. The Nikon waits on his lap. There are whole mountains lined with them down there, Douglas fir, Englemann spruce, the wind breaking in their crowns, each a palace of needles.

Pigeon

Chloe Aridjis

She tried to straighten her thoughts, give them some order and linearity, and when that didn't work she tried to imagine herself elsewhere, on a mountain or coast far from the city, rather than on the Central Line with its erratic movement and office-bound passengers and the prickly silence of those torn from sleep. She and her mother had been lucky to find seats; at that hour the tube was nearly full, a geometric overload of skirts and suits, and wherever she turned she saw freshly combed hair and painted faces and newspapers and briefcases all vying for space.

"You know, you could have died." Her mother lowered her voice in the hope that none of the other passengers would hear.

"Well the point is, I didn't."

"You nearly did."

"I'm cold."

"Don't you have a sweater in your bag?"

"I gave it away."

"You gave it away?"

"This morning. To one of the nurses."

With something close to nostalgia, N. thought back on the small room she'd just left behind, its itchy grey blanket and sweat-faded sheets, and the dent in the wall, courtesy of a former patient, in which her own fist had fit perfectly. Now that she'd left she found herself missing the kind female voices that roused her each morning, voices that for a few seconds invoked the promise of a new life, voices she preferred to that of her mother. And she thought back too on the strange dreams she'd had, dangerous and ornate, dreams unlike the ones outside. And then the wallpaper: red and white stripes connecting floor to ceiling, heaven to hell. There was a window, always locked, but as a view N. preferred the walls and the ceiling since they didn't present any mocking beyond.

In the seat in front of her sat a boy wearing headphones. She hadn't heard any music in five weeks, she realised, not a note. As soon as she got home she would listen to... everything. Thousands and thousands of songs. She'd go through them all, one by one, day and night, an endless carousel of memories, welcome and unwelcome, round and round, that melodic loop of acceptances and rejections, tiny triumphs and huge disasters. In the clinic, what she'd feared the most was the loss of her memories; now, she was willing to keep them all.

"Which sweater was it?"

"Hmm?"

"Which sweater?"

"Just a sweater."

"I hope not one of the nice ones I bought you last month."

She shrugged.

"They won't be on sale again. You won't have one like that again."

She shrugged a second time.

"She must have been a very nice nurse to deserve a sweater like that."

"Yes, she was nice and kind and brought me tea whenever I wanted."

"Shouldn't they do that anyway?"

"Well, they don't."

Her mother shook her head and mumbled something to herself, as if running a few mental maths, trying to assess whether she had possibly, in this latest guilt venture, been taken for a ride.

N. looked down at her hands, which had nearly recovered their delicate form. There'd been a point when she hadn't recognised them, they were so purple and swollen she feared they would break off and drift away, the palms puffy and indistinct, a fortune-teller's nightmare. And then she wondered, as she rubbed them together, what had happened to her gloves, a beautiful pair her grandmother once knit, dark blue with grey borders. They'd begun to feel tight so she'd stowed them away, but where? Well, it didn't matter, what was gone was gone. Just as long as no one touched her records, the only belongings N. swore to herself she would never sell off. This past year everything, pretty much everything, had gone up in smoke, part of an amazing alchemical transformation of base metal into gold.

She couldn't help but keep an eye on the doors. Instinct. Each time they opened and closed at a station, an opportunity came and went.

At the next stop two men clutching paper bags from McDonald's got on. The carriage filled up with the tantalising smell of french fries.

"I'm cold and I'm hungry."

"I'll make you something when we get home."

"That's ages away."

Her mother looked up at the map on the wall. "Only twelve more stops."

"And then the bus."

"There shouldn't be traffic at this hour."

"I don't see why we couldn't take a cab."

"A cab would've cost the same as a day at the clinic."

"Then think of all the money I'm saving you by leaving now."

"I just hope Dr. Reid knew what he was talking about when he said you were ready to come home."

Coming home: once upon a time, quite a while ago now, this phrase was like a magic potion, but the word 'home' had now been attached to so many spaces, it'd lost all currency. Each year it had referred to somewhere else, to a different scenario, a different roof, a different set of faces: the rented flat in Bow, the rented flat in Seven Sisters, the family house in Mexico before her mother went off with the Englishman, and of course the string of clinics where she'd been sent after the first so-called intervention.

At Oxford Circus half the carriage disembarked, leaving room for the dozens of passengers who clambered on. Nearly everyone found a seat and those who didn't grabbed onto the bright red poles and handrails as the tube began to pull out of the station. N. rubbed her arm and thought back on the handsome new patient who'd arrived at the clinic two days earlier. She could still visualise him perfectly, ambling down the corridor with his combed-back hair and long-sleeved turtleneck, no track marks visible, only the familiar scent of melancholy. It was his fourth time there, the nurses said, and they doubted it would be the last. He'd looked over in her direction once or twice, at least she thought he had ... If her mother hadn't arrived so early that morning they might have spoken.

"Twitch, twitch, twitch," her mother interrupted the reverie. "Twitch twitch twitch. I thought they'd ironed all the twitches out of you."

"I set some aside for the journey home."

Yes, her mother had tried. But only for a few months and not hard enough. Her attempts were half-hearted, mechanical, and she'd been careless – forgetting to dispose of expired medication, leaving earrings and banknotes within view, passing on phone calls that should have been screened: endless temptations for the easily tempted. She hadn't tried as hard as some of the other mothers, at least according to the stories people shared, and she certainly hadn't been very present in the early days, when N. had desperately needed her.

It was at Chancery Lane that the pigeon flew in, right into the carriage in a clean diagonal sweep, a whisk of all four seasons compressed into one. It was a large pigeon, slate grey with reddish eyes and white-tipped wings, and it entered at the last possible second before the doors banged shut and the tube recommenced its journey.

One moment it had been on a vaulted platform with friends, the next, it found itself alone with the other species inside a closed space in motion. Almost immediately, with the first awkward movements of the tube, the bird turned into a dervish of feathers, panic and confusion. People ducked and dispersed yet it still managed to graze a few heads and shoulders. Two startled young women rose from their seats and hurried to the opposite end of the car. Someone waved a handbag.

The pigeon flapped this way and that and N. caught a glimpse of its underwing, of an inverse serenity, light powdery grey. Each stroke of its wings released a slight breeze, the breeze of hundreds of flights across the city.

"Sssss," someone hissed when the bird came too near.

After about a minute or two of useless histrionics, the pigeon seemed to calm down and landed on the floor with a thick, clumsy thud. It surveyed the area and then headed enthusiastically in the direction of the men with bags from McDonald's. One of them stamped his boot and muttered something in a foreign language.

The pigeon backed off.

N. and her mother watched on. The other passengers watched too. No one spoke, no one moved. All eyes were on the bird.

At St. Paul's, a station N. rarely used, a woman with a dark ponytail got on and took an empty seat near them, straightening out her skirt as she sat down. The woman pulled a novel out from her bag, cracked the spine wide open, and turned to the first page. When the pigeon pecked at something near her feet, she simply moved them a few inches to the left without looking up from her book.

When had she last read? She couldn't remember. She'd started countless books, of that she was sure, novels and biographies and even some poetry. But despite the warm glow that came out of the pages she would doze off before long and find herself, hours later, with the book in her lap or at her feet, and she'd put it aside and pick up the next one, and this too, she realised, was an endless carousel, though instead of a whole variety of memories the main memory the books brought back was of herself as a student before she dropped out of university, and of her prodigious concentration, remarked on by everyone, and her proud rows of 10's.

Swoosh, swoosh. The pigeon was back in the air and had begun flapping more frantically than ever. It circled a pole, zipped down the carriage, zipped back near where N. and her mother were sitting. People would hastily make way for it, clearing a path for its desperation, but it didn't want to see. At one point mid-tunnel it flew into a darkened window and was thrown to the floor for a few seconds before resuming its flight.

At the next station N. grabbed a sports section that had been left behind and tried to usher the bird out but it grew even more flustered and headed in the opposite direction just as the doors were closing.

"He prefers it in here, where it's warm," someone said. No one laughed.

At Liverpool Street a serious-looking man in a pinstriped suit strode on and sat directly across from them, the aroma of McDonald's replaced by the confident reign of cologne. The man was hefty, with cheeks bearing the flush of countryside and pale blue eyes that with one glance sized up the other passengers. He set down his briefcase, wedging it between his polished black shoes, and unfolded the newspaper he had under his arm. Soon all N. could see were shoes, large knuckles and knees and the outspread wings of the 'Financial Times.'

"By the way," her mother turned to her, "We've decided you're going to Mexico for a year."

For the first time since her last fix, she was aware of the blood circulating through her body.

"A year?"

"You're going to live with your father. We've discussed it and agree it's the best option."

"I'm happy here."

"You know you're not. This is your last chance."

There'd been many last chances; she was nearing the end of her supply.

"What will I do there?"

"You'll live with your father and start thinking a little more seriously about the future."

"Of course, the future ..."

Little by little, it had come to represent nothing more than a shadowy road lit by fireflies, lined on either side by the silhouettes of people and possibilities that would remain just that: silhouettes.

The woman reading the novel let out a small cry. The pigeon had flown past a little too close, brushing her cheek. In a delayed response she waved a hand in front of her face and leaned back as far as she could but there was no need, it had already flapped away. A grey feather zigzagged to the floor.

"Three more stops," said N.'s mother.

It was shortly after she said this, N. would never forget, that the pigeon flew right into the centre of the "Financial Times." Without blinking, the man in the pinstriped suit lay down his paper and within what seemed like a fraction of a second, grabbed the bird – the whole carriage was now watching – and with his fat knuckles snapped its neck. It was a clean snap, expertly done, as if he'd been snapping birds' necks his entire life.

One second the pigeon had been tense and aquiver, the next, an immobile lump of grey. Whatever its journey across the city had been, it ended here. The man deposited the corpse on the empty seat next to him, picked up his paper and continued to read.

The act was met with silence. Everyone simply stared at the dead bird, just stared and stared, as if pooled together the intensity of their gaze might resurrect it.

For a few seconds N. fought the impulse to pick up the pigeon and take it outside to bury – the sanitation people would surely just toss it in a bin – but the thought of touching the thing made her queasy. She imagined what it would feel like to hold the feathery corpse, still warmed by its recent life force, and wasn't sure what was more overpowering, her distress at witnessing such brutality or the guilty flicker of revulsion she'd begun to feel.

As if in quiet defeat, the pigeon's head lay to one side like the emblem on a fallen coat of arms. Its eye had almost immediately turned white, or perhaps it was the eyelid that had closed, and its legs, already stiff, looked like little pink twigs that could easily break off.

N. turned to look at her mother, who continued staring at the bird, willing her to say something, anything. But no, she kept whatever she was thinking to herself, hands in lap, fingers interlocked.

At the following station, which was open air, the businessman folded his paper, picked up his briefcase and stepped out. The doors of the tube took a few moments to close, and as they stuttered N. gazed out at the sky and the platform and the spaces in between, seized by the urge to grab her bag and run for it, in whatever direction opened up to her. But she remained in her seat and with one strong tug unzipped her jacket, for the temperature inside the carriage suddenly felt very warm.

Early

Lucie Whitehouse

Silently, aiming for weightlessness, Eleanor moved to the edge and lifted the blanket. The parquet floor was chill underfoot. She skirted the end of the bed, feeling with her hand for the protruding corner responsible for the yellowing bruise on her shin. Behind her, the shape beneath the blankets made a sound between a sigh and a groan, and turned over. She held her breath, thinking she was caught, but he only sighed again and buried his head deeper in the pillow. The steam heating grumbled in sympathy.

The door was ajar and in the slant of light from the next room she picked her clothes from amongst those strewn across the rug. She dressed in the relative sanctuary of the bathroom and ran her hands through her hair. There was no comb in her bag; she only had what was in it when she'd answered her phone in the library, keeping her voice as low as possible. She'd packed away her books and come straight over. Her hair didn't matter, though; no one knew her here. Contact lenses were more important but she didn't have those either, and her glasses were in Manhattan, eight stops away on the C train. Well, things would have to stay hazy for the time being.

He'd dropped his keys into the shallow dish on the counter last night and now she picked them up, threaded the one for the front door off the ring and slipped it into her coat pocket. Shouldering her bag, she quickly scanned the room, then turned the catch and noiselessly let herself out. In the hallway she exhaled. There was a dull ache in her head as if someone was squeezing her temples between thumb and forefinger.

In the lift – the elevator – she held the key in her pocket, stroking her fingertip along its serrated edge. In a few minutes, she thought, ten or fifteen at the most, she'd be making this journey in reverse, taking the lift back up. She'd use the key and open his door for the first time. Perhaps he'd be awake by then, making coffee. Perhaps, it occurred to her suddenly, he might think she'd gone, walked out without saying goodbye, but he'd see the breakfast things and laugh. They'd eat and then go back to bed. Or perhaps, exhausted, he'd still be in there when she got back and she'd leave the breakfast in the kitchen, drop her clothes on the rug and get under the blankets again. She'd mould her body around his, pressing her breasts against his back. Her fingers would be cold on his skin.

Opening the lobby door, Eleanor stepped out into a sudden trumpet-blast of light. She closed her eyes tightly and opened them again, seeing only the outlines of the trees and houses opposite for the seconds it took her pupils to adjust. When they did, she was dazzled again, this time by the sheer beauty of what she saw. Spring: in the eight hours since their third Martini and the shivery stumble home, spring had arrived.

For almost a month now, banks of filthy ploughed snow had bordered the streets, and the pavements – sidewalks – had been strips of greasy ice stained by cigarette butts and dog shit. Day after day the city had gone to work under an inscrutable grey sky. In a matter of hours, however, the long spell had been broken and a rinsing sun bore down so keenly on the piles of dirty snow that they seemed to shrink before her eyes. She could hear running water – she heard it before she saw it. It was sluicing down the gutter, clean and rapid as an alpine stream, making a lovely, bubbling music as it flowed down the drain. Tick, tock; tick, tock: the beat came from overhead as water dripped from the trees and the scaffolding on the building next door. Overhead the sky was so intense and perfect a blue it resonated in her chest.

It was still early, at least for a Sunday, and there was no one else on the pavement. A single car, one of the huge ones she'd only seen in films before coming to America, was cruising up Lafayette Avenue past Ralph's deli on the corner, Simon and Garfunkel trailing from the driver's open window. Eleanor felt a fresh awareness of her foreignness and was thrilled by it. Everything was new and filled with potential. Things were just starting.

Last week, the night she'd come to Brooklyn for the first time, they'd passed a great-looking deli and bakery. Marafioti's: the name had been written in gold across the window. She'd find it, she decided; that was where she'd get the sort of breakfast one should eat at the beginning: butter croissants, cinnamon rolls, pains au chocolat, freshly-squeezed orange juice. Smoked salmon and eggs for scrambling. Coffee beans, ground to order. The coffee was one of her favourite things about New York. Round the corner from her apartment on Minetta Street she'd found a café that did the best she'd ever tasted; she was going to take him there when he came to her place. When would that be, she wondered. This week? She'd come here all three of their nights so far.

She crossed South Portland Street and carried on down the hill. There was a bagel place on the next corner but no Marafioti's. It couldn't have been on this side of the street, though, she thought now, because they'd been coming the other way, from Park Slope. She remembered how she'd pressed into Eric's side and he'd pulled her round for a kiss.

Waiting to cross Lafayette, she saw a tiny Asian woman – Japanese perhaps – standing on the pavement opposite. She wore a pair of Hunter wellingtons and a chocolate-brown quilted jacket of the type that looked ludicrously hunting-and-shooting in England but contrived to be chic in New York. Her age was hard to judge but Eleanor guessed forty. Her hair, still raven, was cut in a crisp bob.

The lights changed and Eleanor started crossing. The Japanese woman, however, didn't move. She seemed distracted by something but, glancing down the street, Eleanor couldn't see much. What she did see as she got nearer was the red and white striped bag in her hand. Marafioti's was written across it in gold.

In London she wouldn't have done it, but New York had made her bolder. "Excuse me," she said, stopping and pointing at the bag. "Could you tell me where I'd find that shop?" The woman looked at her, eyes wide, and Eleanor felt obliged to explain. "I don't know the neighbourhood – I'm new here."

The woman stared a moment longer and then seemed to focus. "You're English," she said.

"Yes. I'm here studying – at Columbia."

The woman nodded, as if that was satisfactory. "It's a little way," she said. "I'll show you." Her accent was almost American but, not quite.

"Oh, you don't need to show me," Eleanor said. "If you just tell me, I can ..."

The woman shook her head, suddenly adamant. "You won't find it." She turned and started back the way she'd come. A little hesitant, Eleanor followed, hoping it was nearby. The bag of books was heavy on her shoulder. When they reached the end of the block, however, the woman crossed the road again and went on. Embarrassment growing, Eleanor went on, too. She felt as if she should say something but the woman kept her eyes on her feet, seemingly determined to walk in silence. She moved quickly, the bag describing a tantalizing pendulum swing.

They made to cross again and Eleanor decided to tell her not to worry. Just as she started to speak, however, the woman sniffed and Eleanor realized she was crying. She was taken aback – alarmed, even. Standing at the crossing, she'd been intimidating, one of that New York breed whose poise seemed a moral challenge as well as a sartorial one. The sudden vulnerability was disorientating.

Without looking at her, the woman took out a ball of macerated tissue and pressed it against her eyes.

"Are you all right?" Eleanor asked, tentative.

There was silence for some seconds but then she turned. Her eyes brimmed. "I've left my husband." She blinked and two streams ran down her cheeks.

"Oh."

"Just now. I walked out." Her attempt at self-control collapsed and she broke into violent sobbing. "I still bought breakfast – I didn't know what else to do."

Eleanor looked round wildly, trying to think. A little way up the street there was a place with benches outside. "Would you like to sit down?"

The woman shook her head savagely, bob swinging. "He never does anything for me." Her voice was choked, too loud in the peaceful morning. "When he comes home tired from work I always pour him a beer but if he's home first, he never pours me one. I have a job, too, and I cook and I clean and I look after his mother." She sniffed hard. "She lives with us."

Eleanor was bewildered. How had the morning taken this abrupt turn? "Is that difficult?" she tried. "Living with his mother?"

The woman shook her head again almost as fiercely. "No. No, that's not difficult. It's my husband – he doesn't care about me." She sobbed again and then thrust out the paper bag. "I could do this every day – buy his food – but I don't. I cook everything – every meal. I cook his favourite dishes, it takes so much time, but he doesn't even notice."

Into Eleanor's mind came a memory of Eric pressing his face into the pillow as she'd picked up her clothes. "What does he do?" she asked.

"He's an accountant – we both are. That's how we met, when we were students." She pressed the tissue to her eyes again and swallowed. "He was good-looking and clever – the best one in the group. And he chose me."

She gave a half-smile, remembering. "But now he leaves me to do everything. What about my career? I'm ambitious, too. And I was the only one who ever beat him in exams."

They'd stopped outside a restaurant and Eleanor watched as melt-water dripped from the eaves to collect on bags of garbage from the night before. Here the tick, tick was arrhythmic, out of step. "Do you still love him?" she said.

The tissue had fallen apart irretrievably now and the woman wiped her eyes with the back of her hand. She looked up, defiant. "Yes," she said. "Yes. I love him."

All of a sudden, Eleanor saw her mother standing at the kitchen sink with her back to the room, her shoulders shaking. Eleanor was standing next to her, watching as small circles spread across the surface of the dishwater, one after another. Saucepans were piled on the counter. "Have you talked to him? Sometimes people don't even know what's wrong."

The woman looked at her, waiting to be convinced.

"My parents met at university as well but after they had us, my father seemed to forget my mother. She was a great cook, too, and he ate everything she ever put in front of him but to him it was just fuel."

"So what happened?" The woman's eyes narrowed.

"She never told him it pissed her off." Eleanor shrugged. "Just started hating him for it instead. They're divorced."

The woman drew herself upright and sniffed hard, as if trying to re-inhale her dignity.

"All right," she said. "Okay. I'll try. I'll try to talk to him." She looked at the bag in her hand and without another word or backwards glance, she dived across the road.

When she'd disappeared, Eleanor looked around and saw that Marafioti's was on the corner: they'd come right to it. Through the window, the baskets of pains raisins and croissants were so golden they seemed varnished. Her appetite, however, was gone.

Seeing herself reflected in the glass, she took her book bag off her shoulder and held it in her arms. Through the window on the other side of the building, the subway entrance was visible. Holding her books tightly, thinking about how the sunlight would look as it streamed through the library windows, she walked round to it.

The ground was trembling with the approach of a train into the station but she paused for a moment at the top of the steps. The drain at the pavement's edge was partially blocked by a sodden cardboard box, and, its progress impeded, filthy water was churning beneath the grate, threatening to bubble up and flood the street. Eleanor hesitated just a second but then reached into her pocket, took out the key and dropped it in.

Saving Agu's Wife

Chika Unigwe

"So Yaradua goes to Israel on an official trip. He gets sick there and dies. His entourage is told, 'Well, you've got two options. Your president was a Muslim and so must be buried quickly. We can bury him here at no cost to you since he was our guest, or you can take his corpse home but that would cost a lot. Thousands and thousands of dollars.' Yaradua's men beg for a few hours to think about it. Five hours later they come back to the Israelis. 'Well?' the Israeli president asks. The head of the entourage clears his throat and says, 'Your offer is very generous but we'll turn it down. Thing is we all know the story of the famous someone, the son of a carpenter, who was buried here and who rose after three days. We don't want to take that risk!'"

The laughter that filters in from the kitchen distracts her for a moment and she shakes a lot more salt than she intends to into the simmering pot. A raised voice says over the laughter, "That's not right. Muslims are not buried. They are cremated. For their sins, they are burnt. You've not told that story well." The voice is loud in the way people are when they are drunk, but the words are not slurred, so she is sure whoever it is is not drunk, which surprises her, the amount of beer they have been drinking. She can't say whose voice it is. All the men sound alike. That's what this place has done to them, she thinks. It has made their voices the same, almost as if they were clones of each other. Their stories are not that different either. They have all escaped from something: religious riots, poverty, deadend lives, and are hoping to resurrect now. But the resurrection is a farce. The promise this place holds out never materializes. Some have, like her, university degrees, but those degrees mean nothing here. The men hold down jobs picking strawberries and harvesting chicken gizzards. They will do anything but clean. "That's a woman's job," Agu said once when they saw a vacancy for a cleaning job at a time when neither of them had work. It would emasculate him to do that, and how could she have thought he would apply?

"Why do you want to spoil a good joke?" another voice asks. She recognises this voice. It is his. Her husband's. Agu's. Perhaps he sounds distinct because she has known him the longest. He has a beautiful voice. No. He had a beautiful voice. Deep. Like Barry White's. Meant for serenading (and indeed he had done a bit of singing) but having been through what they have, it has developed a jarring roughness. These days, he always sounds angry. And really who could blame him? But she has suffered too. He must not forget that. She has suffered as much as he has. Come to think of it, they all have. Every one of them in that overcrowded sitting room with its mismatched chairs and wooden crates that serve as side tables; every one of them drinking out of the jam jars she washes out has suffered. No one can claim a monopoly on suffering. Certainly not Agu. But suffering is not without its lessons. Here she has learned thrift. Not the thriftiness of her mother back home in Nigeria, who bargains for palm oil until she gets a good price and then boasts of it, or recycles paper bags until they disintegrate, and laughs about that, but the thriftiness of the marginalised, the dispossessed. The sort of thriftiness impossible to laugh about or boast of. Hers is the thriftiness of those who stick to their sort, those who laugh so that they do not have to cry, and pretend it is normal to drink cheap beer out of washed-out jam jars.

Why do they have to be so loud? she wonders, not for the first time today. Everything feels wrong here. Especially the laughter, which is too expansive for the narrow apartment. It must crack the walls and seep into the other apartments and then they would have trouble. Neighbours complaining of raucous voices. "Disturbing the peace," the policeman had said when he came to their doorstep some months ago. How insulted she had felt. Humiliated. Yet she had to smile at the young man, promise they would keep the noise down. Grovelling. She does not want to think about it. And all this talk about Muslims and Christians and burials. The jokes do not amuse her. It feels blatantly inappropriate after what they have been through to laugh at jokes about death. Have they not seen enough of it? The kitchen is hot and she wishes there was a window she could open. It is so hot she feels she is being slowly steamed like the moi moi she has cooking on the other, bigger burner. Moi moi in aluminium foil. The taste won't be quite right, she knows, but there is nowhere one can get banana leaves (or are they plantain leaves?) to steam the bean cake in.

The men are laughing at another joke. She wonders what this new joke is about as she heaves out the bag of powdered pounded yam from the cupboard under the sink. At the beginning, she was unable to eat it, firm in her belief that the powder was not yam, could not possibly be yam, but a combination of chemicals not fit for human consumption. One of the wives, older in the experience of living abroad (and therefore older in the necessary experience of substituting one thing for another), had laughed and told her, "You'll get used to a lot of things soon. This pounded yam included." Now she does not even notice that it does not taste like the real pounded yam of back home: fresh yam, sliced and cooked, then emptied into a mortar and pounded to a stretchy, firm mound, perfect for rolling into balls and dunking into soup. She can no longer recall when she stopped noticing the taste. Or stopped noticing that the perfectly yellow bananas she bought here from the supermarket lacked the sweet, rich taste of the spotted bananas of her homeland. Or that her days had become one monotonous cycle of waking, cooking, and cleaning (not just her house but other people's, young white couples who left sanitary towels and condoms exposed in the dust bins she had to empty, and twice a week an architect's office close to the train station).

Her life has come to this. Her years of study have come to this, her degree in banking and finance from the University of Nigeria and five years' experience working in a bank in Jos, going to her job in power suits and climbing steadily up the ladder. It does no good to think like this, she chides herself, finally dipping her spoon to taste the soup. Hmm, not bad. She had feared that it would be too salty. She stirs in spinach from a can and lowers the fire of the burner. Soon, the men will start asking for their food. She is the woman and must provide for all of them. It's her duty. Her new job.

She lifts the pot with the moi moi off the burner and almost drops it for the heat.

Wiping sweat off her forehead, she makes a mental note to warm some stew for those who might prefer stew to soup. This too is her duty: to anticipate the needs of Agu and his friends. She remembers a story she and Agu listened to once on the BBC. A man comes home tired and hungry from work. He asks the wife for food, but there is no food at home, there's a famine, and so not wanting to see her husband hungry, she cuts off a breast and feeds it to him. The next day the same thing happens. And while she's clearing the table, the husband asks why her shirt is all bloody. She tells him what she's done and he says, "Great! Now we have to start on the children!" Agu laughed and said, "What a silly tale." But she did not laugh.

It was not always like this. Not when they were back home, she climbing the corporate ladder in her coordinated power suits. Then he respected her job, her need to rest after work. Weekends were spent in bed, talking about colleagues and dreams and whether or not to go Saturday-night dancing, and should they start having babies? They had young maids, cousins of cousins, to help with the cleaning and cooking. It was a different life and she misses it. She and Agu were equals then. Now he tells her he wants babies. They should have children. Maybe four. A sensible, even number. And where would they put the babies? In the one small cupboard they have in the bedroom? Of course she doesn't ask him this question out loud. Their apartment has one bedroom, one small bathroom, and an even smaller kitchen, like a toy house. The hallway is narrow and will not hold a baby pram. Where will their children play? Where will they run around and learn to walk?

When she and Agu go to bed in the small bedroom, he holds her tight and empties himself in her. She does not always want to, but she does not resist when he starts making love to her. "Are you on the Pill?" he asks. And each time she says, "No." The only response he wants to hear. The room is not big enough, the space is too limited, for any other answer.

She ladles soup into a huge bowl, careful not to be stingy with the gizzards (special discount from Emmanuel who works in an abattoir) and stock fish (special discount from John who helps out at the Oriental Shop). It helps to have friends in useful places, she thinks, now dishing out the too-white pounded yam into a wide platter edged in a pattern of trellis (bought secondhand from the Web). Even here where it no longer matters, where it should not matter, they still keep away from Ali and Abdul, who are Nigerians, as they are, but of the wrong religion. "The Muslims," Agu would say when asked. "I keep away from the Muslims." As if the Muslims were a highly contagious disease.

"But you can't blame Ali and Abdul for what happened in Jos," she would answer, trying to convince him to return their friendship, their hellos, in hopes of eliciting more than a tart response. "You work in the same factory."

"I can't forget." He lost more than a job in the riots. He lost his faith in his country. "And that's a huge loss," he would always say. He spent his days reweighing the value of everything gone. Agu had a supermarket. On a street full of supermarkets, it was a testimony to his business acumen that his supermarket stood out above the rest. He said it was all down to strategic planning. It wasn't anything he had picked up while studying for his accounting degree (although it helped to have a degree in accounting), it was just that he knew how to place his products so that they caught the eye. The male deodorants with the chocolate bars so that a man who came in with his girlfriend for some chocolate was confronted with the deodorant he might need. At Id ul Fitri, he rewarded his Muslim customers with parcels of ram's meat dripping blood in clear plastic bags, for which they thanked him effusively. Yet when the riots started, that did not save him. Did not save his shop. The name marked him out as a southerner. Agu and Sons (there were no sons, but surely those would come?). His supermarket was razed, and Agu lost everything in one night. All his investment. His will to strive.

There was no question of his wife continuing in her job at the bank. She was marked too.

They cleared their bank account to buy a passage out. No choice. The man who helped them out had only one country he could get them into. Belgium. "They don't even speak English there," she said, wondering what she would do in a country where the languages she knew did not matter. But for Agu it was enough that the place was far away from Nigeria. "I don't care if they speak cat-language. I need to get out of here," he said.

She does not want to think of the corpses she saw the day after the riot. Nor does she want to think of the trouble it took to get them here. Or of the lies they had to tell, the new identities they had to wear. Their passports say they are from Liberia – should she die, the authorities would probably contact the Liberian embassy.

She lifts the moi moi from the pot and places them in a round dish, a present from one of her employers, a lonely woman who tells her often, "No one gets my toilets as clean as you do. You are a treasure." She knows how to scrub toilet bowls until they gleam. Nothing escapes her attention. She is dedicated. That was how her boss in Nigeria described her too. And now how easily she has transferred that original dedication to toilet bowls and wooden floors. How she has adapted to this life she could not have imagined.

She puts the food in a tray, and carefully balancing it in her hands carries it out to the sitting room, where the men are now playing a game of WHOT. The sight of the cards makes her homesick. For a moment her eyes mist and she has to hurry to drop the tray and retreat before they see her like this, but the men hardly look up from their game. When she re-enters with plates and spoons, all four drop their cards as if on cue and Emmanuel (small, slight, with the fan-shaped ears of an elephant) says, "At last. Smells delicious, *nwunye anyi.*" *Nwunye anyi*, our wife. That is what she has become. "Wife" to whichever guest her husband invites home: cooking, cleaning. But sometimes when she sleeps, she still sees herself at the counter in the bank discussing the current economic crisis with colleagues.

Her mother suggested that they move in with her while they looked for new jobs. Agu refused. "I am a broken man," Agu told her. "I cannot begin to pick up my pieces here." But she would have liked to stay back, to try to find a job in another bank in the east. It would have been easy to find something, she had experience after all, but what sort of wife would she have been if she put her career before her husband? And who was to say she could not make a career in the new country? Agu had a plan: he would work in Belgium just long enough to regain everything he'd lost in the North, and then they could move back. Did she not want to see the world? Had she never looked with envy at those returnees who came back at Christmas with foreign accents and wearing the latest fashion? Well, she had, she could not deny it. "Here is your chance to be one of them. Be the one to be envied. Be the one to come back from abroad."

Now they no longer talk about their work. Agu's in the bread factory, transferring hot loaves from one machine to the other (at least that is what she thinks he does, she is not entirely sure), and she no longer talks of vacuuming floors and wiping windows in light tones as if it did not matter.

The words they do not say fill the distance they keep from each other except when there are faults to be found. And some days there are those: when the food is not ready on time, or the house is not tidy enough, or her voice is not wifely enough, and then Agu unleashes his frustrations on her. He uses his hand to thump sense into her. In this way, he has also changed. Afterward he cries and says he is sorry but a man works all night in a bread factory and it changes him.

She thinks, I too have found my way, as she fingers the Pill – several of them, small and pink – in the pocket of her denim pants.

The Circus Safari and Other Marvels

Nikesh Shukla

Dear dad,
Arrived in Nairobi and I'm freezing. I thought this was Africa, but no, I'm wandering around in the hoodie mum insisted I pack for emergencies. It's loud and full of people. It's weird 'cos I'm more moved by poverty here than in London cos everyone here's black and it kinda looks like one of the more sombre parts of Comic Relief. Is that racist? I got my safari all booked. It leaves tomorrow. Tonight, I'm going to a restaurant called Carnivore with some Americans. Apparently they serve ostrich balls, warthog burgers and zebra kebabs. Awesome! Can't believe I'm in Africa! Can't believe you were born here!

———————

Yo dad,
This safari is mind-blowing. We left Nairobi in this army jeep with a trailer behind us carrying all our food. I'm in the jeep with a German pastor who only dresses in orange; her lesbian partner, who lectured me about Baroque music for hours when I told her I play guitar; and this long-haired hippy type called Matthias who's

trying to chat up the American girls. They don't understand his accent at all. Our driver, George, is hilarious. He keeps telling jokes and cool stories about growing up in the slums, and he has all these mad animal anecdotes.

Anyway, we drove up past Mount Kenya to this safari park called Samburu. It's really dry and hot. Better than Nairobi. Finally, t-shirt and shorts weather. We drove into a safari park and immediately saw a sleeping lion. The car has no sides so it was like we were stood right next to this majestic beast. The German pastor woman was sharing all her knowledge about Kenya with us. She's lived here for years and she seems to know/have done everything. She told us how she found lion cubs in her safari tent once, the mother outside growling for them. She had to throw the cubs out of the window to get them out.

Before we got to Samburu, we stopped in this little town, my first rural outing in Africa. I got out to buy some water and ended up getting lost in a market where they sell all these second-hand clothes from all over the world. They still had price tags on them from British Heart Foundation or Oxfam and I realised that these were relief clothes sent out from the UK. All those big containers outside supermarkets that we dump clothes in, they end up here, instead of clothing the locals. I found these t-shirts I had given to a charity shop years ago so I bought 'em for old times' sake. I ended up paying like two quid for them both. I also bought water for the stall cos they kept asking me to buy them lunch as well as pay for the t-shirts. I got back in the jeep and the German pastor was telling me off for buying them water. It was getting their hopes up because the water will run out. I thought she was a Christian. She didn't talk to me for the rest of the day. She told her friend/partner (in German) that salvation was better than false hope. She called me a spoilt rich kid. I didn't tell her I speak fluent German.

So yeah, Samburu park. We were staying in these dinky tents in the plains in the thick of the park with who knows what around us. I had a shower (my first in days) in a wooden shack with no roof. It was weird being naked outdoors, looking up at the blue sky while freezing water refreshed me. We went for a drive that afternoon. I think it was the start of tourist season because there were a lot of trucks and jeeps in the park. All over the place, crawling around like beetles. We interrupted a cheetah hunt. We were sat there in the car, watching these cheetahs stalk an impala and then loads of trucks drove up to see what we'd found. Suddenly, there were ten cars around us, all revving engines, pushing past each other for better views. The tourists with the biggest camera lenses were the pushiest, forcing their drivers to break them through the barrier of cars to get that shot. All we were doing was observing, but no, the people with the cameras seemed to have priority. Drivers were pushing off the tracks and going off-road to get closer. I mean, the impalas, when they saw all the cars and excited yelps and click-clacks of cameras, ran off, leaving the cheetahs foodless and pissed off we had spoiled their dinner, so they just lay down in the long grass till no one could see them.

That night was magical. We sat under the stars and listened to nothing. I found this homemade instrument near the benches and asked what it was. It's called a chamunke, and the guy who had made it (out of old drawers and brake cables) showed me how to play it. The weird German Baroque expert stood over me the whole time tutting at my every mistake. I couldn't really concentrate with her scrutiny so I let her embarrass herself. Then the guy who made it played it to us and it was so magical and beautiful sat there under the stars listening to Kenyan folk songs. I lay down to sleep in absolute silence and absolute darkness, absolutely alone. I had these mad dreams where I was Spiderman being chased by a lion, by a dark figure, by vehicles. I woke up and felt really alone and still and bursting for a piss. I tried to ignore it for ages but couldn't make it disappear, my bladder was swelling with pressure and I couldn't sleep. I didn't really want to walk to the toilet in the middle of the night in case any creepy crawlies got me, or any nocturnal predators ate me. But I was desperate. I unzipped the tent, saw the moon swollen above me like Camembert and it looked so tranquil that I relaxed and felt release and I started to piss. I stumbled forward and started pissing in front of the tent, not hiding myself, flapping proudly in the night breeze. It was the most peace I have ever experienced in my life. The sound of the stream and the sand mixing was soothing. I started to fall asleep upright, transfixed by the stars twinkling at my relief.

Pops,

We just left another safari park and it was horrible. The landscape is sparse, vast and beautiful and yet there are all these white creepy crawlies leeching off the land, spreading petrol fumes. We are raping Africa. Sorry to get all Geldof on you cos you said to me tourism was such a vital part of the economy, but it's ruining Kenya. I know it's like one of the safer countries to visit. It's not like Sudan or Zimbabwe or anything. But the empire never ended. It's strange to imagine you were born here as a child of the Empire, and now, years later, I'm walking around in its aftermath.

We saw some amazing stuff but it's just the way people treat the sanctity of nature. Everyone is desperate to see everything at whatever cost, even if it means driving off-road which is a no-no. But it's not even as if they want to sit there and watch these animals, no, that's too normal. People are desperate for the photograph. They want to spot something, take a wonderful photograph of it and display it on their mantelpiece or screen-saver so they can tell people "Ya, ya, ya, I took that in Africa" (pronounced ahh-frica probably). They couldn't give a toss about what they're photographing; they just want the photographic evidence.

We were driving around this safari park in the early morning. Everyone was tired and we were trying our hardest to watch intently for animals. We turned a corner into a little vantage point where you usually get a really good view of the whole park. There was a herd of elephants grazing there. We all peeked out of the top of the roof and gazed at the elephants. There were four other cars there. More were arriving loudly, clattering into the clearing with no regard for the animals or other cars. The leeches poured out of their roofs shooing us out of the way for the perfect shots. George told us to remain still and quiet as the elephants were looking agitated. We sat down in our seats and watched the elephants out of the windows. One car, without thinking, boasting loud, moustachioed, bare-chested Americans, reversed and nearly hit a young elephant puppy. Its dad stormed over and tried to tusk the car. The cars immediately all fought with each other to get the hell out of there, while the other elephants all stopped what they were doing and started to converge on our vehicles. We left pretty sharpish. I mean, how do you take such little care you nearly run over an elephant? How are you so desperate to keep your tourists happy and snap-tastic, that you seem to forget the basic rules of being a safari tour operator?

"Ya ya ya, now what I want you to do is: be angry, show aggression, move that tusk down a bit, front paw aloft ... show me sexy ... show me Dumbo!"

We heard over the driver's radio that there was a leopard spotted nearby. We asked if we could go see it. George is very diligent and cares about the animals and said maybe we should wait till the crazy rush was over. But we insisted. We had seen everything except a leopard and were really excited. We rushed over to the west of the park and found ourselves at the back of a long queue to see the leopard. The leopard was in a tree hanging out. There were two queues of cars converging in front of the tree and they were having trouble moving out of the way of each other. Plus the people at the front weren't moving anytime fast and were clicking away, trying to get the perfect shot.

We waited patiently, then decided to drive away but we were blocked by cars in both directions. There was no choice but to wait it out. A truck tried to inch forward and lost control, nearly careening into nearby grazing elephants. The jeep in front of us broke down and had to be towed away. Eventually, on the other side of the tree, we looked back to see 17 cars all snapping away at this beautiful, majestic, bewildered creature and its cub, while the mauled leg of a dead gazelle hung off the branch they lounged on. Their tails twitched and claws tensed with every click, whoop and red-faced tourist cry of wonder. They sat patiently while we took our turns snapping away. We're supposed to be bringing the world closer together, when all we're doing is sitting in our cars being life tourists, not experiencing anything unless it's reflected through media. I lived this because I photographed this, I saw this because I blogged it, I'm friends with her ... on Myspace or Facebook. The internet, the availability of information, nothing being a mystery, it's all driving us apart. And we sit and we look at a wonder of the world and we marvel and we worry about whether we got a decent photograph. The circus safari.

Nearly home. Can't wait to see you guys and show you the photos I took of your old stomping ground.

On our penultimate night, we drove through the desert and George stopped so we could watch the sun set over the flat desert plain, dropping off over the edge of the world. It was so red and alive, it looked like a pulsating Strepsil. It was the most serene and breath-taking thing I've ever seen. I have no metaphors or flowery language to describe it. It was just simply truly amazing.

Message to You

Alan McCormick

Message 704

I think it's imagining your hands that keeps me listening: fingers fair and tapered, palms smooth and dry, your sure confident grip sensitive yet subtly sensual. Your voice is a more obvious hook; it's an adulterous voice, full of mischief and bass, a delicious deep tone that offsets your slightly high-pitched laugh when you let yourself go. You like to let yourself go and the people in the studio seem to like it too. Georgina – I know there is nothing between you by the way – treats you indulgently with a niece's cool ribbing, moderating nicely her obvious professional respect for you.

It's time for bed now, Neil. Please think of me in your dreams for I will surely be dreaming of you. If we were telepaths we could share our thoughts too. I send you my thoughts all the time by the way, but as you're a sceptic I'm assuming you don't receive them: I heard you giggling when the Winchester Vicar talked about a frantic ghost in his vestry; that was a bit naughty and if you were here now I would lightly spank you.

I like to imagine your shiver as you react to the 's' word but I'm not a violent person. Let's just say if you were here I'd give you a very good talking to.

Goodnight my love, Rita xxx.

Message 729

That was a marvellous programme today. I laughed when you said that you thought George Formby was "almost certainly from Formby" even though you know and I know that he was absolutely certainly born in Wigan. That tickled the man from the George Formby Appreciation Society and when you said, "ta ta then" instead of goodbye it sounded like you were saying "Rita, when?" I've played it again and again and the more I play it the more I know you are saying it, "Rita, when?" I mean. I've tried a similar thing with your name. I was making T, he who bears no name, a wholemeal sandwich for tea and as I presented it I said it's a wholemeal sandwich with ham. I said "wholemeal" like "Hold me Neil," "Hold me Neil," again and again until eventually he asked me what was wrong.

Message 733

I missed you today. Have you gone and got a cold again? That would be the second of the year. I saw on 'Mail Online' that you and her were out at an opening last night. She might have looked after you better and saved you the embarrassment of being photographed in that awful purple tie and a silly grin I have never seen before, and care not to see again, spread across your lips.

You mentioned her buying that tie seven months ago in a witty (witty on your part) exchange with the gormless weather girl, Katcha. Then you said "thank heavens for small mercies; she might have bought me five ties." Georgina, ever the mock Head Girl, told you off for being unappreciative but you had a point. "Humour," as my mother used to say, "can't hide the truth, dig deeper and it will surely reveal the truth." The truth as you and I know is that purple has never been your colour and never will be your colour. I have sought to normalise the situation by parcelling you up two ties, both Savile Row, both silk, and both navy blue. Please do not return them. All I ask is you rid yourself of the offending tie, along with the pink flowered misjudgement you wore at the Chelsea Flower Show. No need to tell her, I will wager she won't even notice they're gone. I'll be looking out for you and for them, and I'm already flying close to the moon imagining them resting so close to your beating heart.

Get well soon my love, not too many hot toddies, think lemon, rest and dream, my heart is racing, racing its way to you, xxxxx.

Message 735

So, not a cold after all. Gout is painful but surely presents not enough of a reason to be off work? Sorry, I'm worried about you but I'm also a little cross that you've succumbed to a preventable condition through excess. I don't blame you, I don't play the blaming game, but I have to say that someone who swore on oath "in sickness and in health to love and to cherish," to take care of you in plain language, is just not up to her job.

You must know you will need to cut back on the drinking, and, to weather the gastric irritation caused by strong anti-inflammatories, you will need to stick to alkaline foods. I am making you some leek and potato soup laden with double cream and will deliver it later today. I will ring on the bell seven times. If you are not well enough to come down to collect it (I know she will be at her precious work), I will leave it on your doorstep. It's cold and your beautiful tiled steps will be slippery and freezing so please wear your moccasin slippers when you eventually make it down.

I will be there and will only speak if you want me to. I will be wearing my blue Hermes coat. You'll know it because when you did a live recording in Bracknell's shopping centre five years ago, I asked you for an autograph and you said it was "very lovely". You looked straight at me and not at the coat so I think we both knew what you meant. I won't be wearing so very much underneath, and if you ask me in I will gently heat up the soup for you; but if you prefer I'll keep the coat on. I'm bringing the Schubert CD you love, but returned, in case you'd like us to talk less and relax more, and some Perry Como just in case you'd like me to have a peek upstairs. I'll bring two films, *Doctor Zhivago* and *Groundhog Day*, both favourites of yours I know, and will leave the choice to you. I've also bought a large pack of Nurofen Extra in case your foot throbs. Talking of which, I realise of course that you may not be able to wear slippers as it might be too painful. I will bring a pair of T's slate-grey flip-flops if you don't mind wearing plastic. Don't be embarrassed by the look: your natural elegance can carry it off... if not walk it off. Sorry, just my little joke my love, to hopefully ease your pain.

I can't wait, I really can't. 'Till then I send healing thoughts out to you, xxxxxxx.

Message 736

I was so disappointed you didn't answer the door at some point in the day. She came back at midnight as per usual, and after much inspection and poking around in the bag (I had removed the Como and the Zhivago by then) dragged it in. I'm sure the soup was never even served and I know you've decided it's best to keep your counsel, to play safe, but a little drop of politeness, a simple thank you now and then wouldn't hurt you or anyone. Quite the contrary, it would be lapped up and placed in a saucer on the mantelpiece and served up for eternity. No, it's not good enough, gout or no gout, you really should show some appreciation now and then. I will not be taken advantage of.

Well, enough of that, it's still been lovely having you back in my room. I recorded today's programme and have played it three times to make up for the three days you've been away. T came back from work during the last recording and pulled one of those 'pity me' long-suffering faces that make him look like a bloodhound. Then he closed the door and left us to it. I could tell your poor feet were pinching from time to time because your voice went a little high sometimes, and you weren't making as many of your jokes or laughing at them as much when you did. It was so unkind of Georgina to say the only other person apart from you that she knew with gout was W.C Fields. What about Winston Churchill or Reginald Bosanquet? She really is a bitch at times, isn't she? Don't answer, you have a professional relationship to keep up, I'm just being naughty.

Well, it's only seven but I'm exhausted and am off to bed with a good book. I've been continuously reading John Steinbeck after you said you liked him the other day. Naturally, I like him too. I am particularly struck by his thoughts on narcissism: "for the most part people are not curious except about themselves." That certainly doesn't describe me, I couldn't care less about myself, my only interest and care is for you. There I've said it, I can't be plainer than that. It's up to you now. Where do you stand from the point of view of curiosity? Are you hearing my words or do you shut things down and reach out for the off button? Well, I'm reaching out with my heart for you and all you have to do is open up a little... come close and listen, but I won't wait for ever, you can't rely on that, that wouldn't be fair!

Message 737

It must be an omen; a spectacularly good one at that. I came into town on the coach, 737, and then in a taxi via Broadcasting House en route to my doctor's in Weymouth Street. And there you were... wearing one of my ties! I'm sorry I screamed out of the window. That was wrong but I felt delirious, like I was still that teenager screaming at The Beatles in the front row of the Palladium in 1963. I admit I once loved Paul but I can also tell you that I can't bear his stupid plasticine face now!

I saw your sweet gracious smile before you ran in, and may I be immodest for once and shout to the heavens: "The tie really suited you!"

"A tie maketh the man," my mother used to say, and that tie maketh you, maketh you even more perfect than you already are!

There was no need to see the doctor after that. The tie was a sign. It's over. I'll be mature, it's not about winners I know; there are no winners in this kind of thing. I can wait; I know you owe her something. Be kind if you need to. I'll try with T but I think he won't hang on for long; he prides himself on being chivalrous about this kind of thing and would always make way for a better man. Well, maybe he should have the house as compensation as I know you won't be able to commute from Oxfordshire. When she's moved out I'd be happy to move... look at me, I'm running away with myself when I said I'd wait. I can wait. I will wait. Just don't keep me waiting too long!

Reply 1

Rita,
Thank you so much for your kind gifts.
I liked the ties and the soup, and your coat is still lovely!
Neil

Steve-O in Seven Movements

Sean Beaudoin

Steve-O and Mike start playing in seventh grade because Mike's stepbrother is in a band called "Valium Rescue" and sometimes the stepbrother gets laid so why not? But mostly they drink and wear tube socks and have a van. It's fun. They come up with a name, Torrentials, and play hardcore which is not punk and so involves constantly correcting people. Mike says, "Hardcore is to a pickaxe what punk is to lipstick."

There are some fights.

By high school they play a few tiny clubs. Eight bands, all ages mosh pits, low ceilings. Sharpie X's and studded belts. Trying to sound like Fugazi while pretending not to. Mike wears an earring and a Gibson SG. Steve-O, tall and skinny, buys an off-brand bass for eighty dollars. It's called "Bass." The case is lined with fake pink fur that Mike says smells like pussy which makes Steve-O think Mike was lying about all those cheerleaders because it smells nothing like pussy and Steve-O would know since he's been hanging out at Dana Cutler's for months, especially on Sunday nights when both parents work and they can listen to Murphy's Law on her futon.

Mike suddenly decides he doesn't like "Torrentials" anymore. He wants to change to November Regions. Steve-O thinks

November Regions is the lamest fucking name in the history of lame fucking names.

It sounds like a tampon commercial.

It sounds like a free U2 download.

Steve-O threatens to walk, punches a wall, cracks two knuckles. Mike apologises by spray-painting a bed sheet JESUS LOVES TORRENTIALS and hanging it in his parents' garage. There's an anarchy circle around the A. Steve-O has zero clue what anarchy is, or even wants to be. Something about wallet chains and waiters getting more per hour, plus tips. The band begins to round out. A kid named Drew takes over drums, too good for his own good, practices jazz patterns in the middle of songs. Ray Skal is lead screamer, brings sixers of Bud Lite to practice and refuses to share. He looks sort of like Brian Eno, which Steve-O knows because he just stole *Taking Tiger Mountain* by "Strategy" from Record World.

Torrentials have seven songs. Six originals, which suck, and a cover of Thompson Twins' *Hold Me Now*, which sucks. Ray Skal keeps not sharing his beer and going, "besides, they're not really even twins."

They play a couple parties and then a battle of the bands in the school auditorium. After the last song Mike smashes someone else's guitar, sort of like Pete Townshend, except not.

There are some fights.

2

The summer after graduation, Steve-O and Mike do the backpack routine in Europe. Steve-O can't cram Bass into his ancient Jansport, so he takes up the harmonica. It's easy to hit the three notes that matter, and they mostly do blues in E. Any other key means drowning in that chordy Dylan routine even Dylan only pulls off half the time. People stop, watch, walk away. The Euro-cops write Euro-summonses that Mike promises to wipe his ass with later. Somewhere on the streets of Stockholm a guy in a business suit listens for a minute and then yells "You know nothing about the blues! Find another hobby!" Mike wants to follow him, get into it.

"It's bad luck to punch a Swede," Steve-O says, which probably isn't true but keeps them from spending the night in Stockholm Riker's.

3

Steve-O decides to try saxophone. He buys a 1941 Conn alto for a hundred bucks and squonks away in the back yard for a week before producing a single pure note. When he gets to school, an index card on the dorm message board says cheap lessons. The dude is called Tumast. No last name. Tumast refuses to come on campus, says "too many white girls without bras make me nervous." Steve-O goes to his house, a sort of a barn/shack thing. Tumast has three enormous gleaming tenors lined against the wall. He tries to sell Steve-O one. He keeps muting his cell phone. He takes off his shirt and pulls yards of Saran Wrap around his waist, says the sweat helps 'tighten his shit up.' Sometimes Tumast nods off mid-sentence. Steve-O assumes it's just been a long day.

4

In 1991 there was always some prick with a didgeridoo.

5

Steve-O graduates with a degree in pulling the graveyard shift at a motel beneath an exit ramp. Once in a while there's a frugal tourist, otherwise it's speed freaks and pregnant runaways. Authors doing research. Counsellors and their rehab scams. A guy who buys a dozen donuts every morning, leaves the empty box outside his door. There's a cassette deck by the register. Steve-O spins John Coltrane until dawn, the more dissonant the better, like bug spray for the insane.

6

Steve-O buys a beater acoustic. There's a metallic pot leaf on the pick guard. It screams hippie chicks with thrift skirts and anklets. It screams bra-less fatties spinning in the grass. Expectations for an acoustic are so low he's already a step ahead, rumbling through half a dozen Neil Young in front of the campus Quiznos. The kind of girls who hang out and listen hang out and listen. Then a dude named King Ink asks Steve-O if he wants to be in a band called "Scrofula". King Ink insists they'll be the "Guns n' Roses" of the greater Ohio Valley area. By the second practice it's clear they will never be the "Guns n' Roses" of the greater Ohio Valley area, running through the set while the kind of girls who hang around and smoke wistfully kill off another Marlboro red. They do a couple of shows and then one night King Ink orders two large pies with mushroom and extra sausage, goes to pick them up in a panel van loaded with half the band's equipment and never comes back.

7

Steve-O agrees to a weekend roadie with clerks from the day shift he barely knows. Robot, Marcellus, and Gay Don. They camp out one night, hit a titty bar the next, on the way back stop in Columbus to stretch. It's hot and Steve-O's Replacements tee is wet to the shoulder blades. They're at the edge of campus, a strip of dives ten blocks long, beer-soaked carpet and specials in the windows, Jaeger Tuesdays!

"But it's not Tuesday."

"Good point. Let's find a museum instead."

By the fourth place they're shit-faced.

Gay Don starts telling everyone who'll listen they're in a band, mostly because Steve-O brought his guitar, not wanting to leave it in Robot's Camry, which doesn't lock. Gay Don says they're playing The Attic at midnight. A couple girls are like "Oh, really?" not putting much heart in it. The bartender rolls his eyes, cuts limes. Marcellus says they'll leave tickets at will call for anyone who buys a round. Robot runs down the set list, how they do Smiths covers and "Bon Jovi" covers and John Cage covers. How they do "Black Sabbath" covers and "Black Keys" covers and "Black Flag" covers. Steve-O intuits that as the guitar player his gig is to hang back and be silent and cool and superior, one foot on the rail. It's worthy of some sort of paper, sociology or physics, how easily they fall into unspoken roles. Marcellus lead vocals and acne scars, Robot the drummer tatted neck to wrist, Gay Don on eyeliner and bass. They look the part, but none of them plays an instrument as far as Steve-O can tell.

From bar to bar the story gets more honed, more believable, less believable. Robot and Gay Don spin the Japanese tour, groupie orgies, drummer explosions, failed label deals. People move closer, buy rounds. A lie stumbled upon is infinitely more believable than a lie presented. Steve-O concludes that being a fool allows others to reveal themselves. He concludes that the power of belief is redemptive and carries a special allure for the perpetually bored.

On the other hand, it's pretty clear they're being dicks. It's a question of how many drinks are required not to acknowledge it.

"We don't get some back-up singers on our rider soon, it's time for a new manager," Robot tells some underage girl.

"Bullshit," says a hard waitress, two sticks of gum and a tray resting against her hip. "What exactly is the name of this supergroup again?"

Gay Don looks at Steve-O, mouthing oh fuck.

It's worthy of an entirely different paper, this one on the mathematics of sheer dumbassedness, the fact that it hasn't come up yet.

"Yeah, man, what is your name?" says the big dude in a Tupac shirt who bought the last round. Doubt flares. Conversations stop. There are maybe twenty people in the bar, a group of sports guys with backward caps and team sweatshirts, a few townies and metal dudes wristing foosball. Steve-O can feel an undertow, an ugly gravity, an inevitable beat-down coming. For some reason the entire room turns to him, leaning on the guitar case with half a glass of someone else's beer.

"We are ... Crustimony Proseedcake."

It's the first thing that pops in his head. *The Tao of Pooh* had been on the nightstand of the last girl he hooked up with, a redhead who shot a killer game of nine ball. He'd read a few pages while she was in the shower.

There's a prolonged silence.

Sun blares under the half-door, causing the rubber floor mats to steam.

Even the jukebox cooperates, skips during 'Turn the Page.'

And then Robot smashes a bottle on his forehead and yells, "PRO-SEED-CAKE! ALL-RIGHT!"

Solved.

Out come the vodka shots. Out come the backslaps and air-jamming. Every ten minutes someone new walks in and the entire bar yells, "Pro-seed-cake!"

Crustimony hits two more places, adding groupies and acolytes and believers and sceptics and chemistry majors and homeless artists and lab assistants and lacrosse team wingers by the block. It's late afternoon. Everyone is very drunk. Steve-O has just been in the bathroom with a woman who has horrible breath and after a minute says, "no no no, my breath" and pushes him away, stumbling back to where her friends sit on a broken ping-pong table. The music pounds and people dance and then it's time to leave, everyone promising to come see them that night.

"Sound check at ten-sharp, y'all," Robot says, one last salute at the door.

All the way back to the car they laugh, barely able to stand. It's a running guy-hug. A shoulder-squeezing, unbalanced affair. They punch and slap and checklist through the afternoon's triumphs.

"Is there really even an Attic?" Marcellus asks.

"Fuck if I know," Gay Don says.

"And can you believe this character?" Robot says, arm around Steve-O. "Pro-Seed-Cake? That was, seriously, a stroke of genius."

Marcellus agrees. "You pick something even a fraction less weird and we were gonna get stomped."

"First rule of performance art," Gay Don says. "Always ride the wave until it hits shore."

"I dunno," Steve-O says. "You can only fuck with people so long, you know?"

"Wrong," Robot says. "You can fuck with them forever."

They get back in the Camry and drive home.

8

Steve-O is thirty and he's never going to be as good as the guy from the Strokes, let alone Charlie Parker, so what's the point? He sells his electrics, a beautiful '85 Les Paul Studio and a '73 Strat Thinline, for next to nothing. He sells his amps and speakers and heads and pedals and straps and cords and tuners for even less. He donates the sax to an elementary school. All that's left is the acoustic, which Steve-O plays for his three year-old daughter Rose, who loves to dampen the buzzing strings with her tiny palm. Rose especially digs Slims *Family Affair* and doesn't seem to mind that Steve-O always fucks up the changes to *Mr. Porkpie Hat*.

"Daddy?"

"Yes?"

"Daddy?"

"Yes?"

Rose likes to start a question but never knows how to finish. For a second Steve-O thinks that's a pretty good metaphor for every string he's ever plucked or song he's never written.

But then decides that's just more arty bullshit.

"Daddy?"

"Yes?"

Her little mouth trembles, desperate to force out something of value. Steve-O can tell that by the time Rose is fourteen she'll cut her hair at an angle across her jaw, dye the tips purple, get a nose ring. She'll have posters of bands that don't exist yet above her bed and a leather-pant boyfriend. She'll crash a car and burn

down a bodega and spend freshman year teaching herself to play
Souixsie on the trombone.

She's got the time, she's got the genes.

She's got the jones.

Steve-O tries not to be jealous, fails.

The Story of
Our Nation

Joanna Walsh

Tomorrow morning I will get up and again begin work on the story of our nation.

The story of our nation will be heroic. It will also be domestic spectacular pathetic operatic comic tragic tragicomic. The story of our nation will have acrobatics close-ups magic tricks panning shots kabuki marching bands and ice dancing. There will be Gorgeous and Realistic Scenery, an Original Soundtrack, Reflex and Precision-Based combat with Manual Blocking and Dodging. There will be Tons of Enemy Types including Huge Prehistoric Creatures, there will be Item Enhancement. There will be First-Person Mode, as well as many other Modes. There will be drinks and ices at the interval (of which there will be several).

In fact the story of our nation will involve everything. But, as yet, we are only at the research stage. At present I am working on hedgerows. It is a delicate job, and painstaking. I count each leaf and measure it. In spring, new leaves appear and must be categorised differently – by colour and dimension in their pale and unfurled state – to the same leaves as they manifest in full green, and to the tough dark leaves they become in September, amongst the hawthorn berries. So that objects in the world will now load in more smoothly, each morning I make an early start. The weather this month is mild and, like most clients (for we, being of this nation, are those too), I take breakfast to work. There is a stop for coffee at 11am, and at 1pm lunch in the field kitchen. The atmosphere is jolly. There is camaraderie. We are comrades. Because of improvements, inviting other characters into a large group in a different zone will no longer cause desynching issues. Or perhaps it's just the season, or the knowledge we are doing something good, in it together, one nation under the groove.

Some days I start even earlier. I'm not the only one. Walking before dawn I can't see the people, just dark shapes passing dark houses - only the landing lights on – in a silage of cheap perfume. Albanian voices, Polish voices: they're the ones will work 'antisocial hours', which must be recorded just the same as daylight ones, though, having newly arrived in the country, some of them do it for sheer love. As do I. I use weekends to catch up. I like the mornings best. I wake early, drink coffee, revise the week's work, though, while I am working I am distracted by recording what happens those mornings. They're so good, I wouldn't want to lose them. The nation wouldn't want to lose them.

My job is a good one. The hedge fund ensures fair pay and conditions. Even when it rains, the rate and size of drops doesn't bother me; I am not in the water department. I am one of the lucky ones: others count the cracks in concrete, monitor bad air levels at junctions, size up the marble chips in industrial flooring. Still others measure shadows, clock them to time, test their density, calibrate the light that arcs night ceilings through the slits between curtains, the slats of blinds: light from cars, from street lamps. Some measure the gaps between doors and doorsills, the colour spectrum of hair on cutting-room floors. Somebody has to do it. Negative or positive, mass observation is observation of mass and, though this will be our nation's story, it will not be fiction: we have to keep it real. Strictly.

We had books, of course, before, and magazines. We had movies, we had TV shows, also the internet. There, stories were parallel but not the real thing. What was missing was bare fact. So we were taken from jobs at KFC, the BMA, the IMF, the AA, MSN (and HP), the RAC, the RAF, and TGI Fridays, from work in HE, HR, PR, IT on PHDs, on MBAs, on GCSEs, from departments handling production and distribution. There was enough stuff already. We had it all: white goods, brown goods, green belts, grey areas, thin blue lines, yellow perils, red mists, you name it. We knew in our hearts it was time to stop making any more. It was time to sit back and look at what we'd got.

After work, in the evenings, our results are shown on TV. I watch nature programs, mostly, as that's my field: the volume of water in our national rivers, the collective weight of the nation's sheep, the mean hue of the pink part of daisies, broken down by state. I also have a side-project (such hobbies are encouraged). Each night I count the hairs on my head. The result is sometimes even (oddly, perhaps, more often, odd). I record the results in my personal log. My height and weight are noted each morning. I will not be forgotten. When asked for my papers I will present them: the list of diet sodas in my cupboard, the sell-by date of each packet in my fridge, the three sizes of my various shoes, the density of my earlobes in mass per unit volume, everything correctly categorised. I ensure (for instance) that my food is no longer listed in two places in the filters, that it shows up only under "Consumables," that my fruit bowl, where the avocados sulk like slugs, is in a category distinct from the flies that crawl upside down on my skylight (I know their trajectories, the hours of their deaths). I shall wait for approval without fear: nothing will be missing. Everything about me will be remembered.

You know, the only thing I can't bear is, we all change. Like, I used to have a fairly irresponsible job – thorns, if you must know – and there were certain things I wouldn't say to anyone, wouldn't think of saying. But, now I'm in hedges, I've grown, blossomed, and there are things I'll say, quite casually now, sometimes involving cussing even (but in a friendly way, naturally) knowing that now my words will be received in a friendly way, even the cuss ones, though I know they wouldn't have been before. And now I know they might even be received in a friendly way by people who don't know I have the job I have now, because I have things that job has brought me, like confidence and a certain degree of social ease. And when I meet some of those people who knew me from before, they double-take, not because I'm doing the job I'm doing now, but because I'm doing it with comfort as though I'd always done it. I want to tell them, I didn't mean to change.

I don't intend to change any more.

I live alone. It's been that way for a while, and I think it will continue. More change would be too much to calculate. How long is forever? How deep is your love? – what scale, what increments would I use? What chance would I have with anyone else when I still know so little of myself? It is necessary that such encounters have improved stability. More must be recorded if I am – if we are – to count for anything. After all, to know you is to love you ... or is it, to love someone else you have to love yourself? Or maybe it's just, know thyself? Though with that thy I stop thinking of myself immediately, and instead think about who would use such a word, and wonder if they're in some play.

The story of our nation will not be like some play. Once all the data is inputted, there will be scenes you can no longer walk away from, scenes in which you will no longer revive. That's as it should be. There will, equally, and oppositely, be scenarios in which it is possible. This will prevent you from getting your quest into an uncompletable state. Completion is only a matter of time, and time is a One-Time redeemable Item. To give it to another character, you must deposit it in your shared inventory, accessed from major cities. To delete a character when this Item is in the inventory means it could be permanently lost.

In the story of our nation, nothing will be lost. The story of our nation will be entirely true, and it will be a good story, despite its being true. Whatever we find the truth to be, it is impossible that it should be otherwise than good. It will be better than history, updated and analysed each moment for everyone to view. Though not synonymous with, it will be identical to the truth: once we input all the figures you will be able to see everything in a flash and, at the same time, there will be overviews, there will be breakdowns, there will be footnotes, and there will be headlines so that everyone will be able to comprehend the greatness of our nation which will be suddenly cohesive, like one of those ads that shows all the races mixing then the camera pulls out so they form a the giant letters of a single word, not even a word, something more instant, conveying feeling as well as meaning – a logo, perhaps.

When it is all done, what shall we do? Or – no – there is no reason to think about that: it will never be done, it will always be doing. Once we reach a certain level, it will continue to do, even as we watch ourselves doing it. And that's the joy in it, though always to be thinking about the story – which is to always be thinking about thinking about the story – will be such a tremendous effort that is will be difficult ever to be light about it, which, sometimes, is what the story of our nation most requires. How wonderful it would be to stop thinking, or rather, to pause from thinking, to turn the story inside out like a glove, and lay it seamy side out, if only for an instant. How painstaking, what delicate work. But, look! There. It's done, and with hardly any effort either (except that the two types of gloves I have are (1) sheepskin 'driving' gloves, that I do not use for driving, but which nevertheless have ridges of external decorative stitching, and (2) rubber gloves, which have no seams at all). Whatever. The story of our nation needs these sudden turns, I could say *volte face*, but I might be straying beyond our national remit.

Being, myself, on the inside, I could cheat – one leaf's as good as another – but I've only occasionally been tempted to fiddle the figures. No, not when the girls in information check my stats against the pale bulk of my body, but to fix issues as, when performing a new filter, the page is reset to page 0, or where the map will not zoom properly, or to clarify tooltips so they better reflect the correct key presses after rebinding the associated keys. I've never given in to these temptations. My job – our job – is only to observe. Even to measure is to move, which implies, also: to disturb the dust, to make waves. To minimise this we have been issued with rubber gloves, with wellingtons, with waterproof trousers, with mudguards, with condoms. We have been issued with hairnets, fishnets, falsies, gas masks, hygienic paper toilet seat covers, cling film. We will change nothing, not even by being there.

The motorways lie quiet.

Nothing new is made.

Only nature we cannot stop. And thought, if that's a thing.

Changes of season are the most difficult. Yesterday the spiders appeared (where do they come from?) Just past midsummer they lay trails from branch to branch suspending shields visible only by their live centres. These spiders are brown and stripy. The spiders that come later are black. I do not remember them coming this early before. Is this anomaly or just memoryfail?

In the fields behind the hedge I am presently working on, I can see people stooping to furrows with calibrators and rulers. The scent of hedge-roses has reached its highest concentration of OUE, but I have no need to worry. It's being covered. A swat-team has been flown in to work on the spiders. They are videoed audioed tasted pinched analysed.

I type results into my hand-held. As they are numbers on a screen, there is room for many more, as many as there are leaves on a tree.

One day, when I have finished with hedges, I will turn my attention to horse chestnuts.

The Spaceman and the Moon Girl

Ian Sales

He sits with eighteen of his peers in a room at the Manned Spacecraft Centre while reporters launch questions, most of which could be answered by referring to the press releases NASA has handed out, and he's wearing his best suit; it's served him well for several years, the best he can afford on his USAF captain's salary although he'd much rather be wearing a flight suit or maybe his Air Force service dress, but NASA was clear on the protocol and four of the guys are civilians anyway. So he's trying to show he has the Right Stuff coming out the wazoo, because there're not just the other guys in Group 5 but the Mercury guys and the astronaut groups NASA picked in '62, '63 and '65, and he knows he's going to be compared to them just as much as he will be to the guys sitting up here with him on the dais...

He's there in the "barrel" and his wife, she's back in New York, because this was not an assignment she could turn down, not unless she wanted bookers and editors to "forget" her face; so she's one of half a dozen models striking poses and swallowing insults from a photographer with an ego the size of the Moon because "Vogue" is doing a feature on Pierre Cardin and his space age designs. She thinks briefly on her husband, and maybe he's going to the Moon like the President said – and that's kind of ironic because two years before she modelled for André Courrèges' "Moon Girl" collection – but at another barked order from the photographer she's back in herself, and she's not going to forget it – the metallic silver Lurex tights are scratchy, the long vinyl gloves are sticky under the hot lights, the blue "Cardine" dress with its pattern moulded into the fabric like a goddamn egg box – they say Cardin invented the material with Union Carbide – the dress is heavy though it hangs beautifully, the black vinyl high-heeled boots are just as hot as the gloves, and the hat, or whatever the hell it is, more like a bonnet, she can feel the brim of it tight across her forehead; but at least she's not wearing the one that looks like an upturned bucket. Despite all that, she does feel kind of space age and she can imagine a future where she might wear these clothes while her husband goes to work in outer space.

And that night, she gets a phone call from her husband and he wants her in Houston to set up home, because NASA is all super-family and wives are wives first and nothing else second, unless they have kids, in which case they're mothers too. He's picked out a plot of land on Nassau Bay and he wants her there to find a contractor and oversee building the house while he's at the Cape training to be an astronaut. They fight. She has a career to think of, they agreed she could do this until they were ready to start a family – and she privately accepts she's delayed that start time after time – and if he can go and strap himself to a rocket and get blasted into space, she doesn't see why suddenly he has a goddamn problem with her appearing in 'Vogue' and 'McCall's' and 'Harper's Bazaar' ...

He'll win, she's known from the beginning he will win and, in defeat, she belatedly realises that all along he 'allowed' her this last year in New York because he was so busy with his secret project, that Mach 3 fighter jet, back at Edwards AFB. But that's all over, that's all done; and now? Now he's an astronaut.

The house gets built but she even does that wrong, because she picks a different builder to the one used by all the other astronaut families; and now the resentment lies heavy over Nassau Bay like the oily miasma which pollutes the air from the refineries down the coast. They're the only couple with no children – and he acts like this this means they've failed in their patriotic duty, but she had no intention of ever giving up her career, she married him for love not to become a brood mare for the family name. So they build the house, she moves in and she goes to the tea parties at the Lakewood Yacht Club, and the Astronaut Wives Club's meetings, she's not the only one that had a modelling career though she was by far the most successful, and certainly the longest to resist playing the Air Force wife; but this life, this world, is stultifying, oppressive, and she wants New York back, she wants the glamour and the lights and the *haute couture* back.

So when she hears about the "Cape cookies" and she doesn't want to believe he's as faithless as the rest of them, she flies down there and she struts into the Holiday Inn wearing something by Paco Rabanne that was on the catwalks of Paris only a couple of years before, one of his "12 Unwearable Dresses in Contemporary Materials," but it's not unwearable now; although this particular dress is a Chip-an-Outfit kit from Mass Originals, not that she's ever going to tell anyone, and it looks goddamn space age. There's her husband in his blue NASA flight jacket with its flame-orange Rayon lining, looking every inch the astronaut, sitting pretty at the top of the pyramid, and so he should as they've just announced the crew for the next flight, so yes, he's really going to the Moon. She stands there in the doorway of the hotel bar, and all the press present turn to look at her, and she knows she looks like she just fell out of the future into Space City, where they send men into space every day. It took her weeks to make this minidress, connecting up all the little white plastic discs with metal rings, it makes faint clacking noises as she moves – how space age is that – and she's wearing it over a white shift to preserve some modesty and white pantyhose – and there sits her husband, he's in the real space age, he's going into space, to the Moon.

He jumps to his feet and rushes across to her, and it's all baby baby, I thought you were back home, what are you doing here; and she can see some of the guys and those women they're with are not their wives, but at least he is alone, at least there's no 'cookie' she can see might have been his; and she's starting to feel a bit foolish, that maybe she misjudged him, maybe she put too much credence in rumours, these "Original Nineteen" are not the "Sacred Seven" after all, things have changed. But now there're photographers and this she does know how to do, so they pose and she tells them she had a sudden urge to see her husband and congratulate him, and she makes no mention of the other wives' stories about what goes on at the Cape because it's just occurred to her they're trapped back in Houston by their children, by their lives; and they envy her the freedom being childless should have given her, but up until now she's been too blind to see it.

On the day, she sits on the floor before the television set in the commander's house, while behind her the other wives see to food and drinks for those present, but her husband's only the LMP so all the attention is focused on the commander's wife; but they're both in the same situation, their husbands currently inhabiting a tiny cabin with aluminium walls no thicker than a Coke can's, on a tiny world with no air, a world that can kill in a heartbeat. She's proud, thrilled and happy – they all are, they always will be, to admit to anything else would jeopardise their husbands' careers – although as he's about to set foot on the lunar surface there's not much higher he can go. She knows soon she will have to go outside with the other two wives and talk to the press, so she's chosen her outfit with care. Since Emilio Pucci designed the mission patch, she thought it fitting to wear one of his creations, not that many will realise, a silk jersey minidress in a bold print, but she's not wearing the matching leggings, the other wives nixed that, just tan pantyhose and sandals. She stopped feeling space-age a year earlier when they announced the crew for this mission, she's not been in Space City since, and nowhere near the future, she's not even in the present – all these astronaut wives, it's like the '50s, like the '60s never happened, never mind it's now the '70s. Her husband told her, in no uncertain terms, she was an astronaut's wife and nothing else, and just maybe he can forgive her not wanting to start a family, not just yet anyhow, but she's got to fly straight and get in formation, because he's depending on her, she's his wingman. And she bit back the retorts and put her ambitions on hold and vowed to herself she's going to be "primly stable" while he flies to the Moon ...

Which is where he is now, of course, backing out of the LM's hatch, bouncing down the ladder affixed to the landing leg, and now he turns to the TV camera on the LM, waves and then jumps up, propelling himself upwards using his ankles, because this A7LB spacesuit is keeping him alive but it's no picnic wearing it, with its twenty-one layers – Teflon-coated Beta Cloth, aluminised Kapton, Beta marquisette, aluminised Mylar, Dacron, Neoprene-coated nylon, nylon, Neoprene-coated nylon bladder restraint, Neoprene bladder, knit jersey laminate and Nomex comfort layer – worn over a Liquid Cooling Garment; and the polycarbonate helmet and over it the Lunar Extravehicular Visor Assembly with its gold-coated visor, all made for him at a cost of around $400,000. But if he damages it, it's going to cost him more than that, it'll cost him his life.

On the good green Earth, heart-breakingly lonely and precious in a black sky above the lunar horizon, it's late afternoon and the Texan sun beats down on Nassau Bay, the air is like a glass dish hot from the oven, and she stands outside the commander's house before the world, one of three wives. She's doing her best to be proud, thrilled and happy, though the Pucci's a little loud, but the press have decided she's "quirky" and they like that. She looks up but it's too bright and the Moon isn't visible, and she's thinking about what she's just seen on the television, what's she's just heard on the "squawk box" provided by NASA – her husband the living embodiment of American know-how, American can-do, in a place where nothing can live; and there's nothing quirky about his A7LB spacesuit.

But here in Nassau Bay, this is not the space age – though she has worn the label for years, clad by a succession of designers trying to create the future, she knows the real space age is not in her closet but on another world, a grey and lifeless world.

Once, she was a "Moon Girl;" but she knows now she'll never go to the Moon.

Kids Come Looking.
Kids Come Back.

Iain Robinson

Lily's face was buried deep in the crook of my arm, her knees hitched up onto my lap.

"Why are you scared?" I asked.

"The bears."

"What bears?"

She peeped up at me. "The three bears might chase me."

"They won't chase you." I smoothed her soft brown hair, so much like Lucy's. "There aren't any bears, now let's go outside and get some wood."

Lily pushed herself off my lap and went running out through the open door – we never locked it during the day, despite the dangers. I stopped in the porch to pick up my axe and followed her out. I felt at my most useful when I reassured her with lies, told her that there were no monsters under the bed, no wolves in the forest, no bears.

When I caught up with her she was already by the log pile, shifting eagerly from foot to foot.

"It's just a fairytale," I said.

"Why is it a fairytale?"

"Because it's a story told by fairies to scare little girls."

"Why would they want to scare me?"

"To stop you being naughty. Is this a good log?"

She nodded her approval. I stood it on the block and split it with two blows, the sound bouncing off the rocky outcrop that ran along the other side of the valley – crack-crack, crack-crack. Somewhere, beyond the fell, a guard in his watchtower would have looked up, maybe scanned the horizon with his binoculars or through a gun-sight. I tossed the pieces of firewood, clanging, into the bottom of the wheelbarrow.

When it was full I wheeled it into the cottage, Lily's small hands pressing into the small of my back to help me along. We stacked the logs in the space next to the wood burning stove. It was enough to see us through the next few days. The log pile outside would only last another month or so, but then, if we were still there, I would have to take the axe and the saw into the woods and try to find the coppiced trees and fallen branches. I emptied the grate and built up the fire.

"What'll it be for lunch?"

Lily looked up from her dolls. "Beans and maggots."

"Beans and maggots it is."

She did a little dance, letting the dolls drop. "Really?"

"It is your birthday."

"It is my birthday." She seemed to weigh the words in her mouth.

Three years old. I'd found the dolls in an abandoned car, hidden them away. I would have wanted to bake a cake, but the chickens hadn't laid and we needed to ration the sugar, save the flour for bread. Beans and maggots was our name for tinned baked beans with sausages. We were down to our last box. We ate what we could scavenge or grow. We'd lived off beans, courgettes, and tomatoes in the summer. It was autumn, and I had pumpkin and chestnut soup constantly on the go. It was too soon for the winter crops, the parsnips and turnips. The chard was for wintering over and I was using it sparingly to boost our vitamin levels. Jams and chutneys made from the fruits picked from the hedgerows and the woods filled the cupboard. It would be a lean winter, but we'd survive.

I placed the beans and the soup to heat up on the stove.

"What do you want to do after lunch?" I asked.

"Can we go to the river?"

"Why do you want to go there?"

"To fish."

"Is that all?"

She didn't answer straight away, but stood up on her stool to help me stir the beans.

"That's all, Daddy."

We hadn't been to the river for nearly three weeks, even though on our last trip we'd come back with a brace of fish. I don't know where the children had come from, but I found Lilian with them where I'd left her playing on the sandbanks, a boy and a girl, the girl maybe nine, the boy younger, both emaciated, their clothes slack around their middles and short on the limbs. They ran as soon as they saw me. I didn't get a good look at their hands and faces. Lily didn't remember what she told them. I watched her carefully for the next few days for signs of the infection, but none came.

As I dished the food I looked through the window. It was a gorgeous day, warm for October, and we might not get another one like this.

"All right, we'll go to the river. But you'll have to stay close to me."

I strapped the willow fish trap to my back. It was bulky rather than heavy. We'd found it mounted on the wall of a barn conversion on one of our scavenges, the most useful thing in the room. I picked up the spear and the bowie knife, for fish or anything else. My gaze drifted over to the corner where the rifle was propped. It wouldn't be needed. Not today. Lily ran ahead, following the path down the side of the cottage, across the vegetable beds, past the chicken pens and the greenhouse, and into the first trees. She was skipping, the hood of her blue coat bouncing behind her. If her mother could see her, I stopped myself. Lucy couldn't see her, even if she was alive, there was no way now to cross the border.

The path wasn't too overgrown. We'd trodden it often enough, and my guess was that foxes and deer passed through using the same route. It was a natural path, one of least resistance over the low rise and down into the river valley. There was a stream close by the cottage. I trusted that for fresh water more than the river. I could trace it up the fell, check for animal cadavers, dead sheep. We'd managed to catch a few chickens here and there, but the sheep just scattered. Even so, I'd see them sometimes on the dark side of the fell, their fleeces like milk teeth biting through the mists.

Suddenly her small arm was wrapped around my thigh. She pressed into me, muttering about bears. The trees were crowding us, whippy nettle stems and brambles thick along the path. I pulled her up onto my hip. The path was thick with fallen leaves, and the nearly bare branches swayed above us, their creaking almost inaudible, the shuffling of my boots in the leaf-mould enough to send pheasants exploding and careering from the undergrowth. The kids would have come this way. I knew they'd come looking. A few days after Lily encountered them I found the greenhouse door forced open, the last of the tomatoes and a few tools missing. They would have followed this eerie path. As we crested the ridge the trees thinned, and Lily caught sight of the silvery waters below, the first sounds of it caressed her, changed her mood, and she was dashing ahead of me, breaking cover. It was too late to call her back.

I caught up with her on the banks. Her shoulders were slumped, her back slightly hunched, an echo of Lucy in a bad mood. She heard me and turned.

"They've gone."

"I know."

"My friends have gone."

I smoothed the crown of her head and untangled myself from the fish trap – relief , guilt, welling up. Everything around me, the conifers and rocks, the flashing waters, the silt and the soft hair beneath my hand, stretching away and at the same time contracting violently onto us. Sudden sickness rushing up in me. The sun glancing off wavelets. I took a deep breath.

Her face was angled up to mine, peering into me.

"Daddy?"

I exhaled and attempted a smile. "It's okay. Let's set the trap."

She nodded, her eyebrows slanted, all business.

I took off my boots and socks, and waded out to where the water was deeper and slower. I placed the trap with the narrow funnelled opening facing upstream, and weighted it with stones. I didn't know how to use it properly or whether it should be baited, and with what. We'd come the next day and check. If there were more fish than we could eat I'd work out a way of smoking them, that much couldn't be too difficult. I'd seen something on TV once. It was strange how trivia ended up as the stuff of survival.

The rifle had been in an unlocked gun cabinet with a few boxes of bullets. I'd found a man and a women lying in bed, a target pistol in the man's hand, the room crawling with flies. There were children's bedrooms, but no sign of kids. Maybe they'd got the infection first, and were buried somewhere in the gardens. But what if it was the other way round, the kids told to leave, not to come back, to look for help.

Lily sat on a rock and watched me wade out of the water. As I dried off my feet and ankles she stood on the rock, craning to look upstream. My heart leapt for a moment, but when I turned to follow her gaze all I saw was a heron on a rock with a beak-full of fish, its wings partly spread, a commonplace for her already. For the first two years of her life we'd worried that Lily had known nothing of nature, only the city, our flat, the noisy hassle of shopping or the rush to and from nursery. It seemed impossible to imagine that it was all still there.

Lucy had been called into work one morning and never returned. She was an immunologist. She was requisitioned, no choice. After that there was only one phone call, perhaps it was all she was allowed. I wasn't even there to take it because I was queuing with all the others for petrol and bread. The answer phone was blinking. *Take her and get out of the city, get far away. Go north and stay away from everyone. Cross the border if you can, that's where they'll draw the line. It'll be a year, maybe two before this thing runs its course. Take care of her. Keep her alive. You can do this.*

Lily stooped over the water, her fingertips breaking the surface. Downstream the water picked up speed, smoothing over rocks or breaking into white water. Most of the stretch was like this. Some of it could be forded, but it was risky. It was a natural barrier, a line of defence. The valley was off the main road, the cottage out of view behind woods and in the crook of the fell. The track we'd arrived by, on foot, five months earlier, was the weak point. I'd felled two trees across it – hoped it would be enough to put anyone off. But kids were kids. Kids didn't know the dangers. Kids come looking. Kids come back.

I'd shared an allotment before the infection. The seeds were the most valuable thing that I'd brought with us. Nearly everything else we'd abandoned as we went north. The petrol ran out seventy miles short of the border and we covered the ground on foot, staying off the roads, along bridleways and footpaths, by map and compass, with Lily on my back much of the time. The border was closed by the time we got there. Leaflets had been airdropped. Anyone approaching the border would be shot. All we had now we'd either found in the cottage, or scavenged along the away. It was the strangest thing. Most houses seemed abandoned. People had fled, maybe across the border before it closed, or maybe to the city hospitals, chasing rumours of vaccines and anti-viral drugs. Even so, I'd watched that barn conversion on and off for a week before going in.

There was still enough time to try catching something. Lily played on the banks while I perched over the waters with the spear. A few fish pushed up the current and I made a stab at them, missing. I knew I had to allow for the distortion of the water, the way it bends the light and make things look out of place, but I hadn't caught a fish like this so far. We'd had some luck with a makeshift rod and line, but the catches were few and far between. I hoped the fish trap would work.

"Silly Daddy!"

Lily had come to watch me. I pointed out the fish as it moved farther away, out of reach.

"Don't be sad," she said. "We'll catch it again."

Her small hand was in mine. The sun was falling, and I felt suddenly uneasy. It hadn't been far from here that I'd found them, the boy and the girl. The evening after I'd found the greenhouse broken into, I had gone out after Lily was in bed, making sure the cottage was secure behind me. I had scouted the ridge overlooking the river. It had taken a while, but eventually I located their little shelter, what looked like the remnants of a play tent, tied up to the trunk of a rowan tree, and half-hidden by a dry-stone wall. I observed them through the telescopic rifle sight. They were curled up together at the mouth of the crooked shelter, dirty blankets piled up around them. The light was fading, but even so the purple blooms of the infection were clear on their faces. I thought I could see the blankets shudder as they coughed. They would have had a week at most before the final fits and organ failures. Out here, without food, it might come sooner. They would get desperate, come looking again. They were infected.

"Let's go," I said to Lily, squeezing her hand. "We'll have a birthday feast when we get back. You can stay up late."

I moved to leave, but she remained rooted to the spot, her eyes searching upstream, to the fields on the other side of the river, back into the woods, then up into my face.

"My friends, maybe the bears ate them."

There was this horror in her voice. You can't disguise real fear. I'd already seen enough of it. I pulled her to me and felt her trembling.

"There are no bears here."

I held her gaze and she nodded to show she understood, but, as we walked back up to the crest of the hill and the trees got denser, I felt fear tightening her grip. She didn't speak. The long arms of the trees were around us and she kept glancing back along the path. The wind was up, the woods busy with the creaking of branches and the tapping of leaves, with shifting, restless noises. We plunged down the path, brambles snagging at my jacket.

"Daddy!"

I scooped her up and looked behind us, uphill. It was starting to rain, a steady patter, not a shower but the sort that would set in and shroud the fell with low clouds. The light was greyer amongst the trees but I thought I saw movement on the trail behind us, quick and fleeting between the trunks. What if they weren't the kids from the barn conversion? What if they hadn't been alone? What if there were others? The path was steeper, and I struggled not to slip on the leaves, grappling stems and saplings with my free hand. Lily was whimpering, her head buried in my chest. The spear caught a low branch and tumbled off my back, onto the path. I continued a few steps, then started back. I didn't want to lose it. The rain was falling harder, smacking bark and branch, a cacophony of little slaps, like applause. I picked up the spear and sensed the movement before I heard it. It was them, crashing through the saplings. There was a rough cry. A sort of bellow. I pulled Lily behind a holly bush.

"Bears," she squealed before I clasped my palm hard over her mouth. Her eyes were wide, staring past my shoulder. The sounds were close, I twisted the point of the spear. Brown pelt. Quick and wet. Steaming in the rain. It stopped on the path, turned to look, and scented the air. A deer. I let out a breathless, painful laugh.

"It's a deer. Just a fucking deer." Relief giddied over me as we watched its haunches and bobbing white tail vanish into the undergrowth. For a moment I wished I'd had the rifle, but then I remembered its kick, the deep shock of it, my fumbling to empty the chamber and reload, the rowan berries spilling red on the ground. The woods lurched as I regained my breathing. Lily hadn't caught the infection, but that was luck. They would have got desperate and come back for her. I took my hand off her mouth and she beat her fists against my chest.

"I told you Daddy. I told you Daddy. They ate my friends." All eaten up in the peaty soil of the fields beyond the river. The rowan berries spilling a bitter blood on them.

By the time we got back to the cottage she was asleep on my shoulder. I settled her on the sofa facing the stove, lit the oil lamp, rekindled the fire, and then put out the light to save oil. I sat in the armchair, still in my jacket, and through the window watched the ragged clouds scuff over the fell. The border was out there, not far beyond the fell, an hour away maybe. Sometimes we'd hear the helicopters patrolling, but they came less now. We could walk out in that direction, approach the border and wait for the bullets. Keep her alive. I was doing that much at least. I gazed out at the darkening fell, straining my eyes for the pearly whites, the fleeces of the sheep. Up there still, against all the odds.

The Girl with the Sausage Dog

Alexander Knights

For two and a half weeks, Leon has known the girl with the sausage dog as "DAX_26". DAX_26 is the one with the big smile that fills most of her profile picture, and, of course, the cute black-and-brown sausage dog with the smooth-looking ears and the slightly helpless look about him. Leon likes the boldness of the photo. And he likes the look of the dog, Nigel.

Now, incredibly, DAX_26 is here in the flesh, standing beside him in the hilltop gardens of the Horniman Museum. They have a connection: they're fun-loving dog people, not unfriendly cat people, and they share a passion for hunting out London's quirkier museums.

If Luce were to read Leon's profile, she'd laugh. But Leon has brushed aside all thoughts of Luce. And Emily too. He didn't even let himself be dispirited by the silences from the girls on the dating site. He honed his profile description, he widened his preferences, and he carried on messaging. The breakthrough came with DAX_26. When she signed off "Carol xx" in message four he knew they would meet.

DAX_26, aka Carol, is a maker. She makes her own clothes, she makes her own cards. Carol is only 26, but she knows a hell of a lot about post-punk music. She seems pleased with his choice of venue just up the road from her house-share in Peckham Rye. Carol loves dogs. Carol is hot.

So why is their first date going so wrong?

They're looking out beyond the leafless trees and the stark Overhill Estate to London's skyline where the Shard is just catching the last of the afternoon sun. It's a holding-hands moment, but they aren't holding hands. Fair enough, thinks Leon, they've only known each face to face for, what, an hour and a quarter? But there was that moment in the museum's hall of stuffed animals. They were both studying a display cabinet with an armadillo, a hedgehog and a mysterious creature called a pangolin all rolled up tight in their little suits of body armour. He put a hand on her arm and she didn't pull away. He felt the warmth of his fingers ease away her gooseflesh.

But now they're outside in the gardens and she's back in that long black overcoat that looks like it belongs to a man. It's not his, that's for sure. Why couldn't he have just carried on holding her arm in the hall of stuffed animals? Why the dumb offer of the blazer? Girls like Carol don't need protecting from air conditioning. Who does he think he is, Sir Francis Drake?

He realises he's been staring at the ground, so he jerks up his head. His dad does that, says Luce. The head jerk thing. Carol is farther along the terrace where the kitsch wooden bandstand overlooks the sloping lawn. She's staring heavenwards, with one arm up to the elbow in a Daunt Books tote bag. She pulls out a phone and Leon worries that she's looking for a missed message. She'll be making her excuses any minute.

He considers her ankles again. They're very white. Leon noticed her ankles before he noticed anything else about her, before he even knew this was Carol. An hour and a quarter ago he was leaning on the rail that leads up to the museum entrance, looking for a girl with a sausage dog. He saw bare white ankles beneath a long black overcoat, he saw black-and-white trainers beneath bare white ankles, but he didn't see a little black-and-brown sausage dog, so when Carol said his name he nearly jumped out of his skin.

They didn't really talk at the ticket desk or in the queue for the cloakroom. But soon after, down with the fishes in the museum's aquarium, the mood improved.

"Can you believe these?" asked Carol, charmed by the seahorses who were using their tiny curled tails to hold onto upright strands of seaweed. "Don't you think they're so elegant?" Leon couldn't get close because of the ebb and flow of kids who pressed themselves up against the glass and left smudgy prints, but he liked looking at Carol's slim shoulders as she knelt at the tank, and her sleeveless orange dress with large, round, pointless buttons on the back that traced the curve in her spine.

Going to the hall of stuffed animals afterwards was the big mistake. Carol's chattiness dried up as they wandered among the glass cabinets of Sussex foxes and scarlet ibis. There's a hulking walrus that sits on a fibreglass iceberg in the centre of the gallery, and Carol didn't really laugh when Leon pointed out its similarities with the warden who sits beside it. And when she knelt to look at a collection of British beetles pinned in ranks by size order, he could hear her suck in her cheeks. By the time they got to the "Animal Defences" display, he risked the comforting hand on her arm, a move that seemed to go well until he fouled it up with the dumb offer of the blazer.

Now they're outside in the chilly February dusk, and Leon's date is sitting on her haunches by the bandstand, phone in hand, ankles lost within the draping overcoat. Walking over, he sees that Carol is looking at the heart-shaped holes cut into the decorative fence posts that encircle the bandstand. She frames a shot with her phone. Electronic click. Image captured. She looks up and says, "One for Instagram", showing him the screen. The colours are faded like a Polaroid from one of his mother's albums, except his mother would never have taken a picture of a fence post with a heart-shaped hole.

"Oh Instagram. Yeah, looks good," he says, and Carol gives him a kind smile, taking his hand as she stands up. The rings on her fingers dig into his. Remember, he thinks, we both like dogs. We both like dogs.

"Yeah, so I didn't bring Curtis either," he says.

"Curtis?" she asks.

"You know, my black lab, Curtis."

"Oh Curtis!"

"Actually, he lives with Luce ... Lucy."

"Oh."

"That's my wife, ex-wife, well, technically wife, but soon to be ex. Just working on that."

"So you're married." The breeze has picked up some strands from Carol's loosely bunched hair, which she tucks behind an ear. My hair has a life of its own, she says in her profile.

"Soon to not be," says Leon. "Soon to be not married. Divorced." He looks across the sloping lawn towards the family home in Crouch Hill. "She got the dog, she got ..."

"Look I get it," interrupts Carol in a raspy, masculine-sounding voice. "Everyone's got baggage, right?"

How can you have baggage? he thinks. You're 26. But he has her attention, so he maybe he should go the whole hog and mention Emily. She might even like that – if she likes cute dogs, she might like cute kids. Maybe they will come back here one day with Emily.

Carol sucks in air like she's just pulled on a cigarette. "Sorry about clamming up in there. Because, actually ..." She blows out. "Because actually those animals really bummed me out. In boxes. All static like that. I know they're Victorian and everything, but ..."

"It's ok," he says. "It's ok."

She pulls at the belt of her overcoat. "It's just that I haven't been entirely straight with you, Leon."

"No?"

"No."

"About ...?"

"Nigel."

"Nigel?"

"You see, Nigel's actually dead."

"Nigel's dead? Jesus! What happened?"

Carol chews her bottom lip and frowns at the clouding skyline. "Well, it was quite a while ago. A year, a bit more, I remember it was just before Christmas, because Christmas was shit. We had to put him down. It was the totally the saddest thing."

"That must have been tough," he says, and checks himself before saying something patronising like, "You must have been very brave."

"Slipped a disc. It's quite common in sausage dogs, if they jump around too much."

"And that's ... fatal?"

"Look, do you know how much the surgery costs?" she asks, turning her brown eyes on his. "And the physio? And Harry'd buggered off to India for God knows how long, and I couldn't afford it on my own. My parents offered, but the point was that I was supposed to be standing on my own two feet. Harry's a dick. We live in the same flat, we have a dog, we're having, you know ..."

"What?"

"God, Leon," she says, rolling her eyes. "What do you think? Do you want me to spell it out?"

Oh, he thinks. Not really.

"S-E-X," she whispers loudly.

"Right."

"Anyway, Harry was always saying we're 'just friends, Carol'. As if we'd just found ourselves living together with a dog. Losing Nigel got to him though." She sniffs and turns away. "Poor Nigel."

Leon worries she might cry. "I'm sorry, Carol," he says.

"Yeah, well, it's no skin off yours. Everyone loved that dog. How's Nigel? Where's Nigel? What's the little tyke been up to this time? Oh God, I miss him. He used to shake if anyone else looked after him but me. Maybe we could have saved him."

Leon should probably say something else consoling but, then again, maybe she could have saved Nigel. These helpless animals we look after. They trust us completely.

Leon rubs his nose. The Shard is in shadow now. Crouch Hill is directly behind it as the crow flies. Not the easiest location to get to, but it had been affordable back when he'd bought the house with Luce. For Luce. It wouldn't have been her choice, she always says. Too small. He bought her Curtis to cheer her up but that just made it worse. Jesus, Leon, there's even less space now. He knocked through as many walls as he could, and then they had Emily.

"Sorry, Leon," says Carol, and the tears are waiting to fall. "It's just those animals, all dead and still like that."

Emily always cries when Leon visits. She cries when he gets there, she cries when he leaves. The only time she doesn't cry is when she's sitting on his lap or he's holding her in his arms.

"You don't hate me now, do you?" asks Carol.

No more tears, thinks Leon. No more tears.

"Leon?"

"What's that?"

"Because of Nigel. You don't hate me because Nigel's dead. You seemed disappointed I didn't bring him."

"Listen, Carol, I've just thought of something."

"What?"

He puts an arm around her slim shoulders, and turns her away from the skyline and the Shard and Crouch Hill, and back along the path to the museum.

"What?" she says again, looking at him sideways and letting a small laugh slip through.

"Just hold your horses and you'll see."

"Tell me!"

"Wait!"

Oh no, we're not going back in there."

"Trust me," he says firmly, shouldering open the wooden door to the hall of stuffed animals and pulling her in by the hand. They skitter through, her trainers squeaking on the parquet. The warden raises his head and eyes them.

"Ok, bear with me," says Leon, patting his blazer. "Almost forgot I'd downloaded this." He draws out his phone and holds it up to the walrus like an offering, tapping the screen. "Ok, hold this."

Carol obediently takes the phone, which shows the walrus fangs and all. "What, you want me to take a photo? Getting into Instagram?"

He thinks of Emily playing on the living room carpet with his phone and taking snaps of Curtis. Only four and already showing an artistic eye.

"No, no, just press that."

She does as he says, and on the screen the walrus suddenly honks and dips its head, then raises its fangs and its entire blubbery bulk. Carol squeals and steps back as if the walrus might burst through the screen. She continues to hold the phone aloft and on the screen the walrus dips and hulks, dips and hulks, on a loop. "Awesome!" she says, and Leon notices a dimple show in her cheek. "Oh my god, does it work for other animals?"

"I think ..."

"This is totally the coolest thing." And now she's by the Sussex fox, who trots proudly round her leaping cubs, now the pangolin unrolls itself and snuffles the air curiously, now the British beetles prize themselves free from their pins and march out of the cabinet. "I love this app!"

Leon almost has to run to keep up with Carol so that he can see what she's seeing. The warden watches them, but Carol's delight is infectious and Leon is laughing and his heart shakes from the sudden exertion. He pictures Emily again, just because it's innocent fun.

Then Carol swivels and the loose ends of the overcoat's belt slap against her waist. "What else does it do?" She brandishes the phone at Leon. "Be cool if it worked on you."

"It's only for the animals."

"Aaaaahhh!" she screams, looking into the phone. "Oh my God, this is hilarious."

The warden shakes his head slowly.

"Shhh!" whispers Leon, widening his eyes.

"But look," she says, leaning into him. He sees nothing, save for the gallery's glowing cabinets and the lifeless creatures inside them.

"Oh, it doesn't work now because you're not in front of the camera. Well, I hate to break it to you, Leon, but the app thinks you're a sloth!"

"A sloth?"

"Yeah, this is brilliant."

Leon catches sight of a hairy creature, blinking from a tree branch. Then Carol skids round and points the phone at the warden in an exaggeratedly covert fashion.

A sloth, thinks Leon. Not a lion?

Carol suppresses a giggle and looks over her shoulder at Leon, tucking back some hair. She nods towards the warden: "He's a barn owl, apparently!" Carol's spinning out of control, like Emily after a pack of Haribo. Better calm her down.

"Hey, Carol, what about you?"

She freezes. "Oh, me? Good point." A pretty flush has invaded her cheeks. She hands over the phone. "Go on then."

Leon raises the screen, but really he's just looking directly at Carol, her straggled hair, her blinking brown eyes, the warmth in her cheeks, the tip of her tongue visible, her chewed bottom lip, her smile. He looks at the phone. There's a Carol there too – smaller, brighter, simpler. What animal will she turn out to be?

Ivan Returns
To Ithaca

Tara Isabella Burton

Ivan did not go home for the summer. There was nothing beautiful about home. He stretched out on sofas in Berlin; he taught English in Budapest; he sat on benches on street-corners that meant nothing to him and scribbled down their names. Sometimes he wrote letters. He signed postcards with the names of hotels he had not stayed in, he wrote to his mother about palaces and his father about museums. He had set sail, he said, to unknown and dragon-haunted places, where everything stopped his heart.

Nothing stopped his heart. In October, his mother telephoned him at three in the morning and told him he was coming home for Thanksgiving. She'd already made up his room. She'd pay for the ticket.

Ivan came from the airport along the East Side Highway, and when the city lights blinked out, and the skyscrapers floored him as they always did with the geometry of their strangeness – they couldn't be three-dimensional, he felt sure; they were trying to trick him! – he pretended to yawn and told himself that he had conquered it all before.

The street-names here meant nothing to him. They were only numbers, uninteresting on postcards, alluding to nothing, and still when the cab passed the corner on 79th Street and Amsterdam his chest tightened, and he did not to think of her.

There was nothing beautiful about home. His mother dried her eyes on his blazer and his father went down to the coffee shop to get Ivan the fruit salad he used to love and outside his window the lights were pink and plastic and the air smelled of bagels and the dog was rolling uselessly onto its side. He showed his mother photographs, and declaimed the legends of his travels across the living room. He gave things Greek epithets; he called things by their foreign names. He hung a panama hat on the back of the chair.

"You've seen so many things," said his mother. "And now you're grown – and of course it's the same here as it always was. You'll be bored of us, soon enough." She sucked in air and waited for him to correct her.

She fussed about the seasoning of dinner; she commented on the protrusion of his collarbones. She worried about the length of his hair and then at last he snapped at her.

At night he could not sleep, and so because he could not sleep he took the leash and wound it around the dog; together they walked in the shadow of Central Park. Everything was still now, quiet and shiveringly familiar, and Ivan reminded himself that right now, were it not for his mother – for the rending of her garments and the beating of her breast – he would be strolling down the Ringstrasse, or the Rue Rivoli. He would be tipping his hat to passers-by and leaving ostentatious flowers on the graves of writers he had loved.

The squirrels stirred the bushes; the moon hit the benches. Streets drafted down toward the edge of the city, and angled in such stultifying ways, and then he was on Amsterdam and 79th Street, and so he thought of her.

He had walked to school this way, often enough, and he had waited here often enough with his mother and with the dog, and so there was no reason that, just because he had kissed her here, it should be this pressed with the seal of her. But here they'd seen a rat scurry under the scaffolding, and so to be chivalrous he'd placed his arm around her shoulders, and then because they were both red in the crossing-light and things were too wonderful for them to speak they walked towards the park and it was there that he'd kissed her. They'd gotten in people's way and been shouted at by strangers and so, gloriously emboldened, he had kissed her again.

Of course, he'd forgotten her by now. Now he was used to foreign girls, expats in hostels, and once for six weeks in Prague, and in any case he had been a child when with her, wading through the pools of their childhood places, and what he remembered was probably not how it was. Catherine was 16, and he was 17 and knew all the secrets of the world; he took her to the Metropolitan Museum and pointed out to her the ruins of the places he would go to, and the broken pottery of the cities he would make his.

They traded stories on the steps and he told her that one day he would be an adventurer. He made her eyes grow wide and then because of the rat he kissed her by the crossing-light on Amsterdam and 79th Street, and across the park the light off the Time Warner Centre gleamed and blinded him, and for a while he mistook it for the moon.

But that was before he had seen and known all things. That was before he had set off, set off to spend college vacations in his friends' spare rooms, avoiding his mother's emails, sending home souvenirs. He thought of writing Catherine, too, but he had done nothing that he hadn't already told her he would do, and so he had nothing more to add. In any case, he doubted she'd open his letters.

The dog barked; Ivan jerked on the leash, but saw that it had been spooked by a rat and so let it whimper. The rat flicked its tail at him; he thought of her.

He had started to walk the old route – up, left, towards Broadway, up the old street, up to his old school, where subway rumbled under the grate and gum puckered at the bottom of his feet. He saw the pizzeria where he used to buy lunch, and he saw the bodega where he would wink and puff out his chest for cheap beer, and when he passed them he saw her, all-conquering on the stoop, asking him if he would take her to the museum.

It was four in the morning; she was not with him. The subway rumbled beneath his feet, and once when Ivan was six he told his mother that the steam from the grate was in reality the exhalation of giants. This made perfect sense to him; this is how it was.

"One day," they'd said, "We'll go together. To Berlin." They scribbled their itineraries on the back of napkins at the frozen-yogurt shop on 84th Street.

The city was so strange to him. It smelled of gasoline, of cooking-oil, of vomit, and it smelled of none of those things because it smelled of her.

The dog barked again, and the moon shifted against the clouds, and then the light appeared long-fingered against the East River; then the trees in Central Park looked like faces, and on 86th Street Ivan pretended – gloriously emboldened! – that if he only crossed the park, that if he only made his way to the Museum, that she would be waiting for him there.

She owned this city. The streetlamps and the light on the concrete belonged to her, and so they became stranger

Ivan took the route he always took. The joggers by the reservoir were echoing off the dirt path; to Ivan, they were the sound of horses giving chase. The false moonlight gleamed again off the skyscrapers, and once he had walked this way with her, and the way was full of dragons.

He walked faster, and then because he could walk no faster he ran. His chest grew tighter; he coughed and spluttered; the dog catapulted itself over bushes and upended garbage cans; he ran towards the great glass walls of the Museum, splattering mud onto his shoes, and in the ricocheting of his heart against his ribs she was with him.

He tripped over the leash; he fell palms-first onto the hill and across the grass, and through the clear windows of the mezzanine he could make out the ruins of the Temple of Dendur, which once he had shown her, and which had once made his heart stop.

He barely noticed the hands that seized on his elbows; they were not real to him. The fingers rifling through his pockets could not deter him. They belonged to a giant, maybe, or a Cyclops, to bandits or brigands; in any case, he only had a twenty-dollar bill.

In any case, the city breathed with her breath and once, in the days he did not remember, Ivan sat with her, his hand in her hand, and told her about how full the world was with adventure, and how Alexander the Great had wept, once, because there were no worlds left to conquer, but he would never get to the point of weeping, because once he set off he would explore forever.

The dog barked – in the aftershock Ivan decided that it had three heads – and Ivan began to clean the mud from his shoes, and when morning came he remembered how they'd sat with their sandwiches at the back of the museum, and how he'd believed that their kisses were the kind that could split apart continents, and that crossing-posts were citadels, and subway-roars were dragons. This is how it was.

'Til God

Polis Loizou

Thanos used to mock Trachoni. Everybody did. He would tease Roxani in class, when they sat side-by-side in maths and he twiddled his compass on the desk, made jokes about her village being full of Mafiosi. Roxani would roll her eyes at the tired gag but the smile would hang on her lips there for a few more seconds all the same. Lips full as peppers. On lunch breaks the other guys would mime pounding her against a wall as they smoked outside, and Thanos would laugh that donkey laugh of his out of duty. But then the noise of his laugh, and the thought of her face, would knock him back down on his knees, and he'd shut his mouth again.

Every time he flicked his knife to a tourist on the seafront, Roxani would surface in his mind. It was as if she was watching from beyond the palm trees, with a raised eyebrow and that pepper-lipped smile.

Now, as if God was real and laughing at him, his parents were driving him to the mafioso village. To be cured – though they wouldn't admit that. The embarrassment clogged up his throat.

Back to rock bottom again,
I'll roam all night with the bad kids ...

Anna Vissi's laments filled the car as his mother turned the volume up. On the other side of the window, the tips of the cypress trees met five metres above the road, vehicles running between them like children at the feet of kissing relatives. Only fifteen minutes 'til God from here. The Holy House would sort him out.

Thanos watched the backs of his parents' heads, feeling like a scolded child. His mother's head was rigid, moved only to the potholes his father seemed hell-bent on hitting. To his mother, Thanos was forever the boy in yellow shorts who sipped milk and rose cordial from a plastic cup. He could not pretend to be the teen on a Yamaha bike, scouring the seafront for British victims to mug at knifepoint. She had a mole on the back of her sun-baked neck, exactly like his. Maybe the theft started there; first genetics, then the red-faced Brits. He wondered if she'd ever forgive him.

His father's neck was hairy. Despite the heat coagulating in the red Toyota, they were thankfully spared the rest of his body. No TV to wobble towards in Y-fronts here, no motorbike to fix outside on the pavement. Instead the grey polo shirt meant he'd doused himself in Joop! as though he didn't have a wife already. The back of his head was fat and sturdy. It said he was the bigger man. Two sons in the army, but this third one, the loser, had to get in trouble with the law. A waster without a girlfriend. Thanos' being diagnosed with diabetes was worse than a death in the family. It meant exclusion from army conscription, it meant feminising his diet. His father would glare at him across the dinner table, but it was Thanos who always averted his gaze when their eyes met.

Outside the car, on that very road, years before, an old refugee woman dropped beneath a tree and succumbed to cancer. That lady was strong, walking to no home with a failing liver. Now there wasn't even a war, yet Thanos' brothers were being treated like heroes just for being forced into national service. Thanos knew they just spent their nights sitting around in the barracks smoking weed, having phone sex with their girlfriends, putting the girls on speakerphone for the other guys to snicker at. If the Turks attacked again, those guys would be dead on a battlefield in seconds.

"Thanos, stop that!" his mother snapped when he exhaled.

So he shut his mouth. It was only a sigh. But since the arrest, his mother had started taking everything he did as an offence to society. He didn't know what she was so upset about, since it was her cop brother who pulled the strings to keep him from going to jail, at her request. But when they settled down to the news one night as a family, eating watermelon and halloumi off the knife, and heard the account of the Holy House of Trachoni for the very first time, it seemed God had answered her prayers. From then on, the Holy House was everywhere; in magazines, in newspapers, on people's mouths – it was the miracle the island had been waiting for.

Thanos smudged the car window and stared at his skinny wrists, which no amount of lamb could fatten. Roxani would never want someone like him, someone who'd stolen his brothers' black olive eyes and strained them to colourless pips. He wondered if he'd see her today, in her village. In the Holy House. The house of an ex-con where God had decided one night to doodle on the walls. In fucking Trachoni.

But his mouth stayed shut. And his mother turned up the air conditioning.

As they entered the village, it was easy to tell which the Holy House was. What was once a dull cube in a cracked village now throbbed with activity. People poured in and out of the place as though Jesus himself was sitting inside it, kissing them one by one on the forehead.

They managed to park somewhere eventually, his dad's Toyota between two Mercedes. Guys in Adidas tank tops, men with white shirts parted to reveal bleached-out chest hair on sun-grilled skin, sun hats, sunglasses, car shades, women with gold earrings, widows in black, mothers with three copper children, D&G shorts and gold crucifixes ... His eyes, watering from the light, flicked the other way. Nothing but dirt tracks and the ageing bungalows squatting over them. In Trachoni, you would think the Turks had only just invaded.

"*Thano* mou, your dad wants something to eat."

"I'll wait here."

"Don't you want food?"

"No, ma!"

He went to where there were fewer people, somewhere cool to rest his head, and came upon a small, man-made cave. He followed the stony path down to a makeshift church, like the kind people used to sneak off to in the days of Ottoman rule. There were icons and candles in tin foil, and only two other people there. One was dressed in black, with dark curls tied at the back of his head. A priest. Thanos walked away, as quietly as possible.

Back in the noise of the crowds buying souvenirs and praying, Thanos glared at the house. So this was where Joseph and Mary had chosen to end their second donkey ride. This plain lump with a veranda, where an ex-con sat with his family, laughing and eating melon. This white block behind the vans selling ice cream, icons and hot dogs. Shoes melted into soft crunching sounds in the dirt and the stench of onions mingled with the scent of thin church candles. Wax dripped onto tin foil. Tin foil glinted. It was like Sundays with his grandma, when she'd tell him about the archangel who came with a scythe to chop the heads off children who didn't behave. Thanos wished he had his knife and his Yamaha now.

In the throng he spotted his mother's white trousers. They spread at the top, giving her entire lower half the shape of a parsnip. If he could somehow take that weight for his wrists ... He studied her as she fought a bunch of people for the hot dog seller's attention, and won. The woman kissed her crucifix with every last bite of a meal, and called every maid she hired a Filipino, regardless of where they were from. "Filippineza," she would sneer – as though the word itself needed Dettol.

His dad stood by a double cabin, patting someone's bloodhound. He could dip a blackcap in his gullet and pull out a skeleton.

Thanos trudged to the Holy House.

Inside, the rooms were cool. Colours shifted in patchy tones until his eyes adjusted. First came the light bulb dangling from the ceiling. Next was a girl with curly black hair holding her grandma's hand. Children were pulled from wall to wall. A flurry of hands crossed the air, made crosses against bodies. Was there even any furniture in this house, or just a congregation? He couldn't tell.

Thanos searched for Roxani, who belonged in that shitty village about as much as he did. He pictured her face in his head, her left hand scribbling Garbage lyrics in the back of her notepad. He shut his eyes and prayed for her to show. She didn't.

But his mother's voice came whispering: "Thano *mou*, aren't you even looking at the drawings?"

It dawned on him then how hushed the house was; how dark the openings to its corridors. Without the gold leaf of icons, without the drone of a priest's chant, he'd forgotten he was in a House of God. He turned his head to a random wall, and ran his eyes along it 'til they stumbled on a donkey; a creamy blob that appeared to emanate from the plaster. One evening, this thing had transpired.

A man, the ex-con sitting outside, alleged to have heard a knock at the door. On opening it and seeing no-one outside, he stepped back into the house to find this same creamy donkey heading for Bethlehem on his wall. That was the story, told a million times by everyone he knew. But this was no donkey. It was too bloated, too full of sympathy pains for the virgin saint on its back. If God had chosen a house in the armpit of Cyprus to be His canvas, He should have taken art lessons first.

In the corner of his eye, Thanos' parents prayed to the Miracle Drawings on the walls. His mother's eyes closed at the sight of Jesus' face, merely suggested on the plaster before her. The whispers on her lips were for his ears only. A simple pale cross had shrunk his father's shoulders. No one seemed to be talking, yet murmurs seeped through the walls, the bodies, the faces around him. Thanos felt his blood pump through his veins. It was a pain, akin to the kind in his forearms when he once tried to lift his brothers' barbells. The candles sizzled his skin, his head, his lungs.

Before he knew it, his hand was on the wall. His finger smudged the bloated donkey, made it spill its creamy guts. He saw his mother's face, as horrified as if he'd knifed a tourist in front of her.

"It's oil," he said.

But she wasn't reassured; she was speechless.

"Are you crazy?" his father hissed. The Joop! proliferated.

Suddenly, it wasn't only his parents gawking with disbelief. It was mothers and widows, and men with white chest hair and double cabins and bloodhounds. The black beard and soft face of a holy man – the priest from the cave – shot up in front of him. He snapped: "Child, do you doubt God?"

Thanos looked down, his blood pumping to the tips of his ears.

The girl with curly hair was watching him. She wore a long white T-shirt with a rainbow-coloured palm tree on it.

The priest carried on reprimanding him. "Are you a Satanist?" he said. "Are you against the God who made you?"

Thanos tried to block him out. The priests were all corrupt, anyway. It was in the news all the time, the money-laundering to Switzerland, pounds and cents lifted from donation plates. Who ever heard of a holy man driving a BMW? All the bishops were waiting for the Archbishop to drop dead, were punching each other out all over the media. They were all far from saints.

With the room's accusations hot on his back, Thanos left the Holy House. The sun erupted in his eyes. As he shoved his way through the praying flock, his arms floundering like those of a blind man who'd lost his cane, he felt the sugar drain from his blood. Flake 99s tempted him from the ice-cream van but there was no way he'd buy anything here. He'd drop into a coma and shut himself out of the Holy House for good before he'd give any money to that laughing ex-con. That Trachoni Mafioso. Faces and hands doubled, quadrupled, leapt between the sparks on the tin foil under the dripping candles. His arms dropped and his eyelids fluttered, Roxani flickering in and out of his vision with the sun, as she raised her eyebrows and smiled from between the palm trees, between God and the blade of his knife.

Cable

Laura McKenna

Her gaze rests on his white calves, strangely insubstantial given the expanse of khaki shorts above. The fabric strains a little with each upward movement. He doesn't seem to notice, just keeps marching up the track, walking pole swinging and dipping in his hand. She can feel a catch in her chest. She is having trouble keeping up.

"Nigel, please ..."

He smiles down at her, his face pinkly moist under the brim of his Tilley hat.

"Come on Val, just this last bit, then it's downhill all the way."

She sucks in through her teeth and carries on. The sun is warm, or so it seems as sweat blooms under her arms and down her back. Around her, the fields are strung out like a botched crochet. Shades of green are interrupted by a thread of grey stone wall, which tacks up and down hills and dips. A farmhouse or two break the pattern, dropped stitches. None of those awful bungalows here she thinks. Not like the west. Not like round Galway and Connemara. No, this time she has to admit that Nigel has picked a good spot.

Val's something of an expert on Ireland now. Been coming for years. Along with Nigel, of course. They have found some of the most delightful little places: places that most Irish people have never heard of. Not the Burren or Killarney or other likely tourist spots, but undiscovered gems along the Shannon, round Lough Erne and down here on the Beara Way.

Nigel had phoned in February. Wanted to know if she had anything doing over Easter. Not for the first time, she was tempted to say, yes, she did. She was going to the Mosaicists festival in St Ives or perhaps Reiki Week in Glastonbury. But she held back. Hadn't she an obligation, really, to do it for Nigel? So, she went along with his plans thinking that maybe, this year, it might not be as bad.

They reach the brow of the hill. The view opens up in front of them, a present. And in the water below, Dursey Island hunkers, black on grey. Val can just make out the top of a pylon.

"There it is, the cable car."

Nigel is talking loudly. He's already filled her in on the highlight of the trip. The Dursey Cable Car. The only cable car in Ireland. 1,300 feet of 1.2 ton cable. Oh yes, she's heard all about it. Nigel is still talking.

"It's a 6-Funitel Jig Back, unusual you know."

Val didn't doubt it. Even at this distance, the whole thing looks pretty precarious. Feeling a little sickly, she leans against the wall of a farmhouse, dotted with statuary of ducks and lambs and a donkey with real turf in its panniers. Val stares, her mouth forking downward before she gives a snort. Then she sees a peacock standing on a gate pillar. Its tail hangs over the edge sweeping the gravel below in a shock of turquoise and shimmery green. Below the farmhouse though, the sea remains a stubborn grey. Nigel points ahead with his stick.

"Onward," he shouts and without a backward glance, heads down the hill.

The cable car station is actually a hut with a tiny office and two toilets. Val pops her head around the door marked "Mná". She returns to Nigel's side minutes later, her mouth drawn tight, shaking her wet hands.

"Typical, neither toilet paper nor hand towels."

The office window is closed. Nigel reads the sign aloud.

"Islanders, animals and cargo get preference over visitors ... The trip takes 15 minutes ... There are six people living on the island ..."

"For heaven's sake Nigel, I can read."

The window slides back. A man. Grey hair, thin red face. An

expression of studied blandness.

"If you're looking to go over, you'll have to wait."

He gestures with his thumb toward a small man who is leading a cow out of a trailer and across the car park to the cable car. They watch as he uses a stick to flick at the animal's haunches. He whistles, sharp thin sounds, sucking air fiercely through his teeth, urging the animal up to the concrete corral.

"G'yup, suk, suk, g'yup."

The beast raises its head, rolls its eyes seaward then back toward Val and Nigel. It cranes its neck forward, lets out a bellow and makes a move toward them, legs scrambling on the concrete. Val jumps behind Nigel, who laughs. The farmer takes control, flicking and tapping the cow about the eyes. The animal backs up, head tossing from side to side, into the cable car. The farmer hops in beside it and pulling the door across. There is a loud cranking noise as the man and beast head slowly out over the sea.

Val shudders. Nigel is even louder. "Bloody hell, I can't wait, looks terrific, doesn't it?"

They find a spot to sit and eat while they wait for the cable car to return. Val takes a waterproof rug from her backpack, lays it on the grass. Nigel unpacks the rolls and thermos. He places two hardboiled eggs on a plastic plate, and unwraps a small packet of sliced ham. He unfolds a camping knife and sets to making up the lunch. Val no longer tries to argue the point about making or indeed buying sandwiches in advance. This is just one of Nigel's little quirks. And it's not so bad. She accepts a cup of coffee from him. In fact, she thinks, this is quite pleasant.

They have a great view of the island and even though it's starting to mist over, it is still spectacular. Two rusty pylons straddle the sound. The single cable car dandles from thick intertwined cables. The swirl of sea below is dark and viscous. Round the coastline, black rocks jag upward lashed by white edged waves. Val squints her eyes and thinks she can make out a ruined building on the island.

"Is that a church do you think?"

Nigel chews quickly, and gulps a bit. "Oh, I believe so. I read somewhere it was ..."

Val gazes back at the island, as Nigel's words drift over her. She can't see so much as a tree or a bush just dun-coloured low grass. The only movement, the distant surge of sheep, looks like maggots from this side. Here the wind is loud even on this mild day as it funnels round the island dragging Atlantic air with it.

Nigel eats with abandon, clamping down on his ham roll, seemingly oblivious to everything but the sensation of teeth and tongue working together. He even hums as he eats. Val turns her head from the sight of the crumbs which land on his fleece.

He was always a messy eater. As a child he caused havoc at the table, spilling his drinks, sticking his elbows into his dinner, knocking over cereal boxes. Their father in particular could not hide his irritation, but Nigel seemed unaffected by it. Why did she always feel that tug of responsibility? Sympathy? Their parents seemed bothered, perhaps even embarrassed by him, by this evidence of their sexual life, born when they were in their late forties and Val already fifteen. They treated him like ... like a curiosity? They seemed fearful of what he might say or do. Val was asked to "occupy your brother" whenever visitors called. On one occasion, Nigel waylaid a guest outside the bathroom and demonstrated the workings of the vacuum cleaner to him for at least half an hour. After that he was confined to his room for social evenings.

By the time Nigel was at college studying engineering, Val had been married and divorced. No children thank God. It was enough having Nigel during college breaks. And to think he's still at college, a senior lecturer. She often thinks she should have discouraged him from becoming so dependent on her, but once their parents died, well it just seemed easier to go along with him. And between times, she had her own life. She kept busy. Her job kept her busy, too much so. Couples' therapist. No shortage of clients there. God it was great to get away from it; the tedium of it, the unbelievable repetitiveness and inevitability of the problems they presented with, you'd swear they were the only ones in all the world. Why she could write the script for most marriages. Most ended the same way, like hers.

Val stretches out, shoves thoughts of work to the back of her mind and looks around her again, hears the waves, feels the furl of grass beneath her fingers. Grounds herself. She reaches for a small spiky yellow plant, bog asphodel. A little early she thinks, pleased with herself for recognising it without her guide book. Perhaps she could keep a wildflower journal. Most people never noticed what was right there in front of them, blooming before their very eyes. It's just a question of opening yourself up to things, to paying attention.

A sheep stares at her as it trips past, its blue tattooed rear swaying, fastidious in its gait. Nigel has moved away and is looking at a sign beside a stile. Frowning now.

"Look Val, it says dogs have been shot here in the past."

He pauses, staring at the words.

"Oh come on Nigel, it's because stray dogs worry sheep."

"Worry them?"

He glances at the retreating rear of the sheep.

Val shrugs, packs her things and waves her arm at him.

"Cable car is nearly back."

Nigel slides the door across. There's a screechy tinny sound, and then a whiff of cow smell or grass or ... Val looks inside. Splodges of wet brown excrement cover the rusty floor. Two wooden benches on either side. She sits down while Nigel fumbles with the latch, a flimsy thing like you'd find on a cupboard. She curls her hands around the edge of the seat. Pasted to the wall is a yellowing sheet of paper. Psalm for Protection. And now she can see what is dangling on a length of twine from a hook beside the window. It's a plastic bottle in the shape of the woman. The Virgin Mary she thinks, judging by the blue crown or bottle top. Quaint, really, these old superstitious ways.

The cable car lurches forward, the pulleys screeching above her. She feels a distinct swaying motion as it trundles out over the ocean. She glances again at the Psalm.

Nigel sits opposite, beaming.

"Mind if I open the window? I'd like to see how this works."

"Yes I do mind Nigel, you're rocking the damn thing."

When she can bring herself to look again, the island seems to be moving toward her, ethereal in a light misty gauze. Nigel is looking at the floor, pointing.

"Look, there's a hole."

The metal is corroded, and through a gap the size of a fist she can make out the sea below. The perspective is odd, disorientating. She pushes herself back on the bench and clasps her hands together. Nigel brushes his hand on his shorts. His booted foot is tapping.

"What is it Nigel?" Val's voice is querulous.

He looks out the window and plucks at his fleece.

"Nigel!"

"See, Val, the thing is, I'm, well, actually I'm getting married."

And he's smiling at her, beaming like he has handed her a precious gift. Val stares. Nigel, married. It simply wasn't possible.

"She's a post-grad student, from Duisberg ..."

She just couldn't imagine it, couldn't imagine him with a love life, and certainly not a sex life.

"... Monika. I think you two will get on really well. She loves the outdoors as well and ..."

Married. She'd actually thought of him as asexual, neither one thing nor the other. Has he had other relationships and not told her or is this his first at thirty-five?

"Val, what do you think?"

The cable car has reached the halfway point. The wind is loud now, rattling the metal, vibrating along the cable.

She thinks.

"Are you sure? It's so sudden."

He laughs now, a ripple of happiness. She feels it, like a lash.

"Oh, no, not sudden. We've worked together for over a year."

The rusty pylon is moving toward her, filling the small window. The island slipping away behind it dimming in the swathe of mist.

"You'll have to come with us now, share our holidays ..."

The cable car cranks under the frame of the pylon and seems to hang there for a long time, creaking, while only the black jagged edge of the island is visible squatting beneath the cloud.

And then it lurches forward again.

The Weakness of Hearts

Kate Williams

The carter left me too early, and I had to walk up the hill, dragging my bags. The house was black against the sky by then, and the moon was covered by dirty clouds. The trees bent over toward me and their look was not welcoming. A squat woman with keys at her side opened to the banging of my door.

"They are all abed," she said. "We were expecting you at five."

I could see nothing past her but a few flickering candles. You would think a grand house like this one might have a chandelier.

"Lateness," she said, as I crammed past her and smelt her, hard onions and coins.

I nodded, as I walked into the narrow hall. What was to say? That the coach had stopped at an inn on the way, where I did not know, and there had not just been a place to eat and horsemen in corners, but stalls, like a fair. There were usual things, pans and vegetables and boxes of firewood, but then grander stalls with flounces, haberdashers" things, hats, ribbons, skeins of silk for pretty girls, ones with calm hair and blue eyes, not me, and piles of cakes and gingerbread for little boys. It was not those that drew my eye. After a lifetime of girls, I had had my fill of sugar. It was the stacks of old books, sitting in front of a man who looked even more aged, his hair so untidy under his hat that it looked as if it had been half torn from his head. Women flocked around the ribbons like flecks of colour on a painting, but he sat there, still, as if not caring that the people around him seemed not to want his wares.

He looked at me and smiled. "Books for you, Miss? Maps, recipes, stories, I have them all. Even spells, if they would interest." I had thought of a story book, when I came close. I had never had my own book, only borrowed time with those of others, and I desired a story more than anything. But then, as he held out one and there was gold on the spine, I could not stop but look more.

"Any spell you might desire, Miss," he said. "Catch a sweetheart, ruin an enemy, kill the evil spirit, chase away the demons."

"Magic is a temptation for weak minds," remembering what the minister had said when he came to investigate a craze for fortune telling at the school.

"All minds are weak, Madam. Some can be made stronger, with methods such as this book."

And I do not know why it was, but it was something about the girls flurrying nearby me, their talk, and not wanting to be like them, never, and I gave him the coins I had saved for so long, over hours and weeks and months of listening to their lazy French and correcting their composition and being laughed at for poverty, and then in a moment, the book was in my hands. "You will find it useful, Miss," he said, bowing a little.

It was then, only after all the flim-flamming around him and the staring that I realised time had gone quicker than I could credit, and I had missed my coach. So I had to wait for another and beg my way on, and use up almost the last of the coins I had toiled so hard to gain. And then I was late and the family were all abed and it was the worst start that could be to my time at Radleigh Manor, which I had for so long seen as the beginning of my freedom. All the way, I clutched the book in my hand and did not open the goldy cover. If I had sacrificed so much for it, I should force myself to make the pages worth their while.

I thought in the cart and decided I did not dislike the notion of spells. Better than religion, those hard chairs they made us sit in, every day, listening to sermons by fat men who ate well after lecturing us. I could not bear that.

The housekeeper left me in a small upstairs room. "There is no one to help you prepare for the night," she said. "But I imagine you are not accustomed to assistance." She was right. I was no girl from a good family brought low by money, and sent out to earn her living. I was an unclaimed child, taken in for the goodness of Mrs Pennyfather's heart, and now sent to Radleigh with a strange moment of luck, a place above my station.

Next morning, I awoke and the sun was streaming through my windows. They had left me to slumber and no one had awoken me. And that is when I knew. There were enemies. I pulled on my clothes as best I could, took myself downstairs, through corridors that wound. A footman stood outside one door, his face covered over with displeasure as he looked at me.

"The family dine there," he said. "Master and his children, that is. The servants have already breakfasted. I imagine Mr Merrycroft will see you in his study after breakfast." He made a move so slight, not even twitching an eyebrow, as if I was not even worthy of such effort.

I waited outside the study, standing up forever although it was surely not even one full hour. Finally, when it seemed to me as if my legs were beginning to bend under me, a tall man came forwards, a woman in uniform with a scraped face behind him, and then two children of about ten or so, both in white, hands resting clasped. I could not tell if they were boy or girl. Their faces were round and there was something not distinct about them, as if they were clay models shaped by infants.

"Miss Glass? We did not see you last night. But now, you can begin immediately with your duties. These are my children, Alfred and Albertina." His hand gestured and I still could not tell the genders. "You will go up to the schoolroom, and begin with geography. On the wall, there is a table of your classes at what time, and you will follow that." He touched one of the children on the head, as if to push it forward, but he or she stayed at its place, resolute.

"I have never seen children who look so alike." I suspect it was uncalled for of me to speak so, but I could not help it. There seemed not a feature apart.

"They are not ordinary brother and sister. Two children born at the same time, from the same seed." The hand that he then rested on their head was not kind, I thought. "They replace their mother. She died to have them."

I held my palm towards the child nearest me. He – or she – did not take it. My fingers rested in the air before I took them back to my side.

"Go," Mr. Merrycroft said. "Thompson will show you the way."

Pinch-face bobbed, and then turned on her heel. The two children trotted after and I began to follow. Up we went, through staircases that wound around and turned and narrow halls that came so close I thought they might fall on my head, and nowhere a window to lighten our way. All the while, the pair of them walked on ahead, their white gowns flickering in the dark.

We came to a door, and Thompson took a set of keys from her skirt and poked one into the hole. It clicked and creaked and the door flung open. I stood behind the three of them and looked at a room that was surprisingly large and full of air. There were even four windows, not unclean, and there were spots of sun on the floor.

"Your room, Miss Glass," said Thompson, and then before you would know, she had shut the door behind her and gone back out into the dark. The two children positioned themselves either side of the window. Their faces glittered next to the panes.

"Geography," I said, hating the quiver of my voice as it emerged. Had I not had worse than this? Whole classes of girls who had laughed and paid no attention and still I had won over them. But I stared into the greyish eyes of these two and felt nothing more than a desire to cry out. It was as if even their cheeks had eyes in, that stared back and mocked. I tried to think of my most wilful charges at Mrs Pennyfather's – Julieta Pilking, who would try to pull my hair, Sarah Bellow, who would sing out bridal tunes at me, for they said I would never marry. And yet I could not make them seem anything but very little, naughty girls who would be wed themselves soon enough.

"Which of you is Alfred and which is Albertina?"

The one on the right shrugged. "We could be either, if you prefer, Miss. Or both."

"I would like to know which is which."

A shake of the head. The other stayed silent, staring back.

"Well, then. I shall call you Alfred and you Albertina," I said to the speaker, thinking that there had been a slight gruffness to his voice. "Sit down and let us begin our geography." I walked to the bookshelf at the end of the room and found it well equipped. I pulled out "The Geography of France" and began to read.

Then, for the next hour, they tormented me. They sat quietly, still, gazing at me with their grey eyes. All the time, I talked of the Alps and the rivers and the large flat area in the centre that only worsened the weather, they stared. If someone had come in, they might see nothing but obedience. But I knew they were worse and more wicked than any of the noisiest Pennyfather girls. I asked questions, but they made no answer. When I put out a question, I listened to the silence and then answered it myself. The minutes on the clock slid by as if time was backwards before it came forwards, and the cruelty was worse than three hundred calling-out Pennyfather girls. At the end of the hour, I walked over to the large plans, written in ink on handsome paper, and then attached to the wall. Each day was divided, in wide, curving script – history, comprehension, mathematics, drawing, art. I drew my hand up to the "A" of Art.

"Who wrote this?" I was almost talking to myself. And then one responded. "Miss Jenner."

I turned and looked, hardly able to credit that one had spoke.

"She came before you," said the one I was sure was Albertina.

My predecessor. I had not been aware. I had thought from the letter I received from the housekeeper that the children had been at school.

"How long did she stay?" I touched the curve of the A once more. It was so thick that you would almost think it just drawn.

"Who knows?" sang out Albertina behind me. "She is gone now."

I suppose they had played her with this dumbness too, this malice, and she had hurried away in tears.

"Where did she go?"

And they both stared back at me, without speech, their faces like white clay once more. The one I was sure was Albertina propped her hands into her lap. I moved my hand down the lessons.

Driven away by these two. I would not be the same. Indeed, I had no choice. I had no family and Mrs Pennyfather would never take me back. I had to make my best of what I found here. If I did not leave here with a reference, I could not think what I would do. No chance of getting further work without a character. I would be lost, and that would be the truth.

So I turned away from the paper and smiled at the two demons in front of me. "History," I announced. "What were you learning with Miss Jenner?"

They gave me no reply. "Well then. The Hundred Years War."

I read out some pages to them about the battles and the politics and the struggle for territory. The valour of Henry V. And then I looked up. Albertina – or so I thought – regarded me with her pale grey eyes.

"Did they have witches in the Hundred Years War?"

"I do not know."

"I heard they did. Men hunted for them. And then they burned them at the stake."

"The flames ate them and then their flesh turned and melted," said the other.

"I know nothing about such matters. I believe there was Joan of Arc, but she did not deserve to die. She heard voices and thought she heard God. But we are not talking of the French, yet. Come. The Battle of Bauge."

"Do you think it must hurt to be burned, Miss?"

"I cannot imagine."

"But then you are glass. You would not burn. You would break into pieces."

I stared at her, and then Alfred next to her, and I could not help it. My legs began to shake. It was the look in her eye when she said, "break into pieces". There was only a flicker, only a moment in the pale iris of her eye – but I knew I had seen evil. It shone out to me, just as clearly as you might see goodness in the kind touch of a nun.

"The Earl of Buchan," I continued. "Let us think of bravery."

At one, Thompson came with trays for their lunch. "You dine with the servants," she said to me. I would not. I would not go to the hall below, laughing girls, mocking me. Instead, I waited and I asked her if she could show me the way to my own chamber. She told me to turn left, then right, right again, along the corridor and up the stairs and around the spiral, and then up and right again. I put her directions in my head, even with her bad sour tone.

When I finally arrived at my room, after all those hours of walking, I threw myself onto the bed. I told myself that I must have courage, but I could not find it. Instead I thought of what the man had said about the weakness of souls and temptation crawled into my mind. Kill an evil spirit. I took the book of spells from my bundle and touched over the gold on the cover. I opened it, and the paper crackled. I thumbed pages of catching husbands or curing children or turning sickness from your body, until I came across the one I desired. Chasing the evil spirit. I ran my hand down the list. The receipe did not look too troublesome. It would leave the patient in a daze for eight or ten moons, and after that he would wake and all bad demons would be chased from his body.

Nothing happened that day, of course it did not. I returned to the classroom and went through Miss Jenner's timetable of mathematics, then comprehension. They would not say or write a single thing. I had weeks of this, and Thompson's sharp face, and the master who brushed past me and the servants who laughed, and it all began to rise up in me, faster each day.

The desire grew and grew and I suppose that was the thing. Alfred and Albertina became for me demons, whose hearts must be prevented from breaking the world around them. Months of their cruelty and strangeness, and I knew then that I had to do my task. When I took one day off, I walked into the village and bought the things from my receipe. I mixed it in my room, balanced the composite parts. I did not feel fear.

Every day, they sat there staring back at me as I read and followed Miss Jenner's timetable, and I thought of how I would return them to goodness, soon enough. I had been brought here from Mrs Pennyfather's for a purpose.

Miss Jenner was in my mind when I put the receipe in their cups. I tipped in the receipe, thinking of her weeping in her room, and fearful of where else she might go. "You may find it useful," the man at the stall had said. The twins would be in their daze, and would remain so, as the evil spirits left them, for at least eight days, perhaps more. I imagined them awaking, usual, sweet children, and how grateful the master would be to me.

Next morning, I woke expecting to hear the whole house in fear at the daze and the sound of the doctor called. But all was bustling as usual. I threw myself out of bed, seized with excitement all the same, found my way downstairs, and every step I took, the noises were only those of the family as usual.

The same footman was there, his eyebrow raised. I could not bear it. I walked past him into the door. Mr Merrycroft, Alfred and Albertina turned to look at me. They stared. I looked at them.

A slow smile spread across Albertina's face, the first I had ever seen. Her eye twitched.

In front of Mr Merrycroft, on the table, was my bundle and my book of spells. And then there was a sound from outside, of men arriving and wheels and voices, and I knew I had moved from an instant in the minds of others from good to bad.

Albertina touched her pale mouth. "I was right, Miss Glass," she said. "It must hurt to burn."

A Religious Experience

Charlie Hill

1

In the house, waiting to go to choir practice, Sheila hears Phil's voice. He is watching telly and going on about it again. He goes on about it all the time. "How could you do that to yourself?" he asks, except it isn't a question, "I mean what kind of mentality is that?" Sheila isn't sure. But then he can't be either. And it doesn't stop him holding forth. "It's all about the Arabs you see. Not having anywhere to live. It's a Jihad. A Holy War."

His voice goes on and on. It is the only thing she can hear. It bounces off the walls of the house, bounces around inside her head. It is all she can hear in her head. There is no room in there for anything else. Sometimes she thinks her head is so full of his voice it will explode.

"There's some do-gooder here," he's saying now, "talking about how it's all in the Koran. It's not you know."

She doesn't blame him. She doesn't blame anyone, except perhaps herself for not being able to blame someone. Because it's no-one's fault, not really, not even his. He's not a bad man. He has never mistreated her, not in that way. And he's always been like this, after all. Interested in politics, in what is going on in the world. When he was still at work he'd talk to her about how the force could be better organised, how their budgets could be better spent, how Community Support Officers were a waste of space. She didn't mind this. It was just what he did. She would listen to what she had to and then he'd go to work and she wouldn't have to listen to any more.

But now that he's retired, it's got worse. He never leaves the house. Just moves from the bedroom to in front of the telly. Sits there and watches programmes about it. So there is more of him and less too. It's as though he has given up, passed sixty-five before he has reached sixty.

And there's no room for Sheila. They have a small kitchen, a small back room. Their bedroom is small. Phil is a big man. He is a big man in a small house and Sheila is smothered. Trapped. His life is her life is his life. There is nowhere for her to go, nowhere she can call her own, nowhere she can be herself, whatever that might be. It is what she imagines it must be like to be in prison. In solitary confinement. Because although Phil's voice is everywhere, Sheila feels as though she is alone.

It's not that she doesn't love him. She loves him dearly. She tolerates his quirks – the way he complains about his tea being too strong, his custard too thick, his gravy too thin, the way he comes to her on a Saturday night, every month – but she loves him resentfully too. She has to love someone and dearly comes easily to her, but the resentment has also been there a long time, even if she has only just begun to realise it. On a Wednesday, when she has choir practice, when just for once he could be quiet, give her a bit of room in the house, give her a bit of room in her head, it's the resentment that is strongest. Because Sheila hasn't given up.

She has been singing in the choir for about four months now. She saw the advertisement in the local paper. She was looking for something to do after he took early retirement. She has always sung. Only to herself, of course. She's not very good. And she's not daft enough to think she is. But she enjoys it. Singing makes her feel part of something. Connects her to the world.

She hears his voice again. "Look at this! Have you seen this? The way they treat their women?"

Sheila needs to tell someone about the way she feels. About the lack of room in her life. About his voice, bouncing around in her head the whole time. It is hemming her in. In the house. In her head. It is driving her mad. But she knows it's unlikely. She can't imagine talking to anyone about it. What would be the point?

No-one would listen. And if they did no-one would understand. She's no good with words. Never has been. No, things will stay the way they are. She will stay the way she is. Hemmed in. Trapped and alone.

2

In Peter's car, being driven home from choir practice, Sheila listens to Peter. It is the longest night of the year and the light is high. Peter is talking about the piece that the choir is singing. It's called *The Dream of Gerontius*. When they started singing the piece, they were told it was about the journey of a man's soul after death. Now Peter is explaining it to her.

"There are many different ways of looking at the work," he says. "People seem to take from it what they want. But there's a thread that runs through all of them. What Gerontius found is that in death – as in life – we can be free."

Sheila hears Peter's voice and it is like music. It envelops her. She is comfortable in its embrace. It makes her feel a part of something. Peter has been giving Sheila a lift to and from choir for four weeks now. She thinks back to the first time. She didn't speak to him about her situation – she'd been right, she couldn't – but there was something about the way he made her feel that made her things would turn out OK, that it would be all right anyway. After he'd dropped her off, he stayed with her, for a week. Every time Phil went on about it, every time she indulged him in his quirks, Peter was there. A presence.

"'I went to sleep and now I am refreshed,'" says Peter. "That's the soul of Gerontius, after his death. It's a release for him, you see. He's been freed from his earthly cares. There's something there that appeals to us all, I think. And that's what's great about the piece. It still has the power to move."

"Yes," Sheila says "yes it does," and this is true. Although she is relaxed, at this very moment she is also stirred. There is anticipation of something. Expectation even. Whether this is because of Peter or the words of Gerontius or both, Sheila doesn't yet know. But something is coming, something good. She can feel it. Now a momentum is building. More words come back to her: "... a strange refreshment, I feel in me an inexpressive lightness. And a sense of freedom as I were at length myself and never had been before," – and as they do Sheila feels light-headed. She is warm but she begins to shiver. Her breaths get shorter and then Gerontius' sense of freedom comes to her and with it a sense of purpose, triumphant and shining, and the car is filled with light and in the light there is a feeling, a great surge of happiness that overwhelms her, a rush of joy that fills her heart until it's ready to burst and then washes out from inside her and over her in a wave of joyous pulsating relief. Sheila is carried away, helpless. She doesn't want the feeling to stop. She closes her eyes again and then opens them and she listens to the music of the words. Then she hears her name – Sheila? Sheila? – and it's Peter calling her and he is saying, "Are you OK?" and then it's over, the feeling passes, Sheila is trembling but it's over, it is over.

Peter stops the car by the side of the road. He is giving Sheila a chance to recover. But Sheila doesn't need to recover. She sits and looks out of the car. They have stopped by a park. There is grass and the light is still high. In the distance there is a row of tall thin trees, waving in the breeze. She's thinking about what's just happened. She's trying to be calm but she's still excited. Sitting here, in Peter's car, it has all become clear. God has come to her. He is with her and she is no longer alone. He has shown her what she must do, what will make everything better. He has spelled it out for her through the story of Gerontius. It is in the words, it is all in the words, the truth of it is as clear as the light in the sky.

She's always thought that to end a life – any life – is wrong. But this is different, she can see that now. This life is no life. And in cutting it short, a soul will be released.

"'How still it is,'" she whispers, as Gerontius did, "'I hear no more the busy beat of time, no, nor my fluttering breath, nor struggling pulse.'" She thinks of Phil. She must pick her moment. It's only fair. It will come as a terrible shock to him, a nasty surprise. How will he cope without her? He'll be lost. Maybe even unable to function. At the same time this isn't about Phil. It's about her. Her fluttering breath, her struggling pulse. Her freedom. And she will be free.

"Are you OK?" says Peter again. Sheila doesn't reply. As Peter drives her home, she sings: "The sound is like the rushing of the wind, the summer wind among the lofty pines."

3

Later that night, Sheila did God's bidding. She smothered Phil with a pillow as he was sitting in his chair downstairs in front of the telly. Phil was a big man but Sheila felt strong. Afterwards she walked to the park where she had stopped with Peter. She sat on a bench by the road and it began to drizzle. The trees across the grass were blurred. She heard the words of Gerontius again and gave thanks for them. She turned her face up to the rain. The drops glistened out of the streetlight and shone in a fine mist and Sheila was there in the raindrops and the mist and the dark forms of the trees, Sheila was there with God and alive in His words and she was alive in the late dusk light itself.

Seen and Not Seen

Reece Choules

Naked on the sheetless mattress, legs apart, arms stretched wide, he watched the clouds move outside his window. There was a knock at the door. Loud. Knuckles on wood, once, twice, three times. He didn't move. He didn't speak. A woman's voice broke in.

"Can I ..."

"No."

"I've made sandwiches."

"Did I ask for them?"

Silence. She thought about this. She thought about the next part of their routine.

"You've got to eat."

"I'm not hungry."

"But Mr. Henry ..."

"I said I'm not hungry."

Silence returned. A breeze came through the window caressing the limp cock hung sadly between his thighs. He turned on his side. She knocked at the door again.

"Mr Henry."

On the embossed wallpaper of the half-decorated room he made out tortured sex acts in the obscure twisted lines and bubbles. He made out faces scarred with horror, grotesque in the shadows of a large floor lamp. Poorly put together. Rarely switched on. He reached with trembling hands towards the face he once thought of as his own.

"Mr. Henry."

"Go away."

"I'll leave the sandwiches outside your door Mr Henry."

He watched a spider crawl along the wall above the skirting board yet to be painted. He had never liked this room. Its angles too harsh and sudden. Ceiling low. It would forever remain unfinished. Forgotten. Lost to the past. He heard the phone ring.

"Tell them I'm asleep. Marta, do you hear me? Tell them I'm asleep. Marta."

He coughed. Lungs flooded with air. He could hear the high and low points of exclamation in her tone, but try as he might he was unable to make out words. If he had been in his own room then, well, life would be different, life would be as it was meant to have been.

Floorboards creaked under the disturbance of footsteps. He could feel her pressed up against the door.

"Mr. Henry."

"What is it Marta?"

It was her turn to offer silence. She took a deep breath. If only she could see his face. If only she could make a connection.

"Marta what is it?"

"That was Mr Bodill."

He turned to face the door. His limp cock fell from against his right leg like a tree. Slapped against his left. This amused him. This childlike awakening of what was there. I am a man. Ugly. Sick. This brought forth a wry smile. This brought pain. Shooting. Burning. Through the deep, permanent creases of his face it throbbed. He closed his eyes.

"What did he want?"

"He say he have to see you Mr Henry."

He turned back away from the door. Stared up at the ceiling. The spider was now crawling above him. In a book he had once read, a man had awoken to find he had turned into a giant bug while sleeping. Why couldn't he fall asleep and wake as something new? A bird perhaps, so he might fly away. A dog, so he could be loved for doing nothing but being there. He tried to imagine himself as a spider. Hanging upside down. He smiled. Once again the pain came in waves. His fists clenched. He slammed them into the bed. He didn't want to wake up as something new. He wanted to wake as he once was.

"Mr Henry he say ..."

"Out of the question Marta."

"Sorry."

"You did tell him no didn't you Marta."

He heard the faint squeal of rubber soles burning in the compression between weighty anxiety and the twisting of foot into floor. He could feel his heart racing. He could feel the beginning of a migraine working its way up from behind his eyes towards its resting place above. She had yet to speak.

"Marta."

"Yes Mr Henry."

"You did tell him I couldn't see him."

Another silence. He thought he could hear her sobs. He watched a plane disappear into white clouds yellowing. He tried to imagine the faces of those on board. Beautiful. Then ripped at the seams. It had been so long though since he had seen a face, his imagination failed to produce anything new. Any sense of pleasure he was hoping to derive was replaced by an overwhelming sense of loss. He sat up slowly. His unkempt hair, longer than it had ever been, fell loosely over his face. It tickled scar tissue.

"Marta."

His voice was low. Soft.

"Yes Mr Henry."

"What did you tell Mr Bodill?"

"I ... Oh Mr Henry ..."

Her words cut out and she broke into loud sobs. He waited for her to finish. That was all he could do. No consoling. No there there. No it will be ok. I am in here. She is out there.

"Oh Mr Henry, Mr Bodill say Mrs Jaar is sick, really, really sick."

He fell back down onto the bed. He put his arms up in the air. Spread his fingers. He closed his good eye. Through the blurred vision that remained he could make out a moving black blob by the loosely hanging ceiling rose.

"Mr Henry."

"Yes Marta."

"Are you ok?"

"You can go now Marta."

"But Mr Henry I ..."

"Go home Marta. I'll tell you all about it tomorrow."

He felt her move away from the door, the creak in the floorboards. Mrs Jaar was sick. Anna was sick. He reached for lips she had kissed. He could hear a child's laughter. Tears welled in his eyes. She's sick. I'm sick. The front door closed.

"Marta."

Silence.

"Marta."

He got out of bed. Twilight rays shone on the tiny handprints made in different shades of blue that neither he nor Anna could bring themselves to wash away. He heard child's laughter. He whispered a name. Took off the dressing gown hanging on the back of the door. It smelled of alcohol and stale sweat. He opened the door slightly.

"Marta."

No reply. He was alone. He pulled the door open. All the lights were on. She had not wanted him to step out into darkness. Too much darkness, she had said. Not enough light. On the floor just behind the threshold a tray of sandwiches, bland, lay under a clear glass lid on top of an expensive plate. He shook his head. Picked up the tray. He could only admire her perseverance. He could only curse her stupid naivety. He stepped out into the hall. He caught her face wrapped in laughter. He had asked Marta to remove all photographs. All mirrors. She hadn't been able to put this one away. The three of them together on what would have been a forgettable summer's day. Anna. A kiss rested on her face. Tommy. Held by his side. Tiny hand pulled apart the style of his slicked back hair. He stared into the eyes. He couldn't bear to put this one away.

He tried to remember the sound of their voices. Silence.

He made his way into the living room. Placed the tray down on the coffee table she had bought one Sunday. Hot. Rancid smells burnt his lungs. Alcohol. Gasoline. Tommy was teething. They had to rub a gel, sweet tasting, over his gums. She said she had to have it. They argued over the price. Price didn't matter. He owed her this. She knew it. He knew it. It was left unsaid. It didn't matter now though. Those principles, that feeling of paying too much, of giving too much, it was all gone. He turned the television on. It was loud. He didn't care. The neighbours wouldn't hear. Not with reinforced walls and floors. Not with social lives. He turned it up louder. It would not drown out the ringing in his ears. It would not drown out the thoughts of her. She was sick. He turned towards the telephone. I am sick. He sat down. Perhaps he should phone Bodill. Tell him not to come. Perhaps he wanted to see him, someone, her. On the television screen mothers gathered outside a church, weeping, crossing themselves, pulling on the uniforms of soldiers, asking them,

"Why?"

"Why my girl?"

They would be told there was nothing to be done. This was meant to be. His will. He picked up the phone. The dial tone seemed to speak to him in its repetition. You deserve this. She doesn't. She is sick. He put the phone down. On the television screen a reporter stood by an accident scene. Grass blew in the breeze behind him. The red and white tape in the distance wrapped around a tree.

"What happened here today locals say was an accident waiting to happen."

From an overhead shot the twisted, crushed, reorganized car lay still at the end of a black trail. He reached for his face. Police were walking in and around the area in organized steps. He pulled away. When they carried him out he was unconscious. Figures in white overalls and facemasks, walked away from the day's carnage with tiny, clear plastic bags. The loud beeps of the heart monitor filled the lonely room where he had slept his dreamless sleep. She sat at his bedside without emotion, keeping her grieving for a place that knew them, where she wouldn't hate herself for those unspoken but known of moments when she wished it had been different. When he woke, to the white walls, to the repetition, she would not be there. It was better that way. On the television screen a beautiful woman in figure hugging dress pointed to different parts of the country.

"Tomorrow's weather is looking quite promising."

So they could predict the future. They could tell you what was in store. No one told him what was to come when she said,

"I'm pregnant."

It was unspoken but known that he didn't want it. Boy. Girl. It didn't matter. He valued freedom above all else. Children were responsibility. Chains. He wanted freedom. To know there was an exit. The decision had been made. It wasn't, had never been, his to take.

"Can't you see Henry, this was meant to be."

And the weather woman said,

"In the North there is a band of rain that will ..."

So they could predict the future. There was no God. There was no reason. This was all just an accident waiting to happen. She was sick. Anna was sick. It was all just meant to be.

"So most of the North will be touched by rain. Moving down to the Midlands the weather will be mild and breezy. And for those in the south temperatures will rise steadily leaving some of you to enjoy a beautiful day."

She was sick. I'm sick. She knew this. She knew this the last time. Rain falling, light sneaking through the cracks in the doorframe, when the knock on the door came. Knuckles on wood, once, twice, three times.

"Henry."

He watched a plane disappear into the clouds. He imagined the faces of the passengers. He reached towards his own.

"Henry."

He had nothing left to say. No more to offer. In her eyes he saw all that was unspoken. Tommy, his broken face, their broken hearts, what was and what could have been.

"Henry don't you at least want to say goodbye."

He could predict the future now too. A knock at the door, loud, unsympathetic. Bodill stood without affection, a bridge too far between them. You haven't been there for her. He would tell him the past is past. There was nothing he could do now. Locking yourself away won't change things. She was sick. She needed him. What good was all this doing? It wasn't your fault. It was his fault though, for he had always been able to predict the future. When she said,

"I'm pregnant."

He knew instantly it was not going to end well. Life would change forever. He would be responsible for another. A God. Unforgiving. Judgmental. He was set up to fail. He knew this because he knew that each life was an accumulation of those lived before it. God was dead now. There was no reason to it. The buzzer rang. He let it ring. Outside streetlights were coming on. Cars were beginning to fill the roads. The buzzer rang. He let it ring. She was sick. I am sick. Tommy was gone. Tomorrow was going to come again. He could predict the future now. He would not wake how he once was. There would be no God. There would be no reason. For some it would be a beautiful day. For him it would be another without them.

Clipboards and White

F. C. Malby

The starched white sheets crinkle beneath my thighs. The walls are white; clinical. The door is pale and open. Beyond it, the muffled voices of people in white travelling along the corridor. I see flashes of clipboards, glasses, and white; maybe jackets. I am not sure why I am here. My head is woolly and my feet numb. Looking through the window, which is higher than usual, there is a meadow of greens and splashes of yellow. Beyond that nothing but sky; grey mainly. I need to wash my hands but they refuse to move, lying heavily, tingling, as though dipped in iced water. I was told to lie prostrate. It's the drugs, they said, just rest.

My mind never rests. One. Two. Three. The tiles above the sink are unsymmetrical. Four. Five. Six. There is no middle groove where the grouting should lie. Seven. The fourth tile should not be in the middle. The lack of symmetry makes me feel uncomfortable and unsettles a sense of order, or disorder, in my mind. I remember, maybe earlier, a doctor in the house, an ambulance, a cup of coffee, a dog and Sandra, in no particular order. Why do I remember Sandra last? Where is she?

She said something about help. I have had the same job for over twenty years and I have an engineering degree. Why would I need help? I pay taxes: twenty percent. I put my children through school: fifteen years times three. I cut the neighbour's grass every Sunday: twenty seven neat strips of green. I watch the news: thirty minutes each night, minus five if I don't feel like sport. I do the crossword in the local rag: fifteen questions last time, three blanks still left. I was head boy at primary school. Why would I need help?

"Mr Ravenstone?"

I am still sitting on the crinkly material. I stare at the coat by the door. It falls lifelessly from the peg as though a person has just slipped out and is due to return at any moment.

"Mr Ravenstone, you need to rest. The specialist will come and see you, rest."

Rest. The word repeats itself in my head. They speak to me as though I might be dead, or unhinged. I suspect that they would not speak to me if they thought I was dead. Are there one or two coats? The clipboards and the glasses leave the room, leave the door open, and disappear into the flashes of movement in the corridor, slipping away like eels into a murky river.

Tick. Tick. Tick. There must be a clock somewhere. It sounds as though it is at the bottom of a bag, which is below me on the floor. It takes some rummaging through items of clothing, which are not neatly packed. They are not laid out in the way that I would fold them and stack them, carefully. Instead they have been manhandled like meat. I can feel the smooth cover of a new book but I do not have a new book, and the bristle of a hairbrush which is definitely mine; I know this from the grip on the handle. A pair of felt slippers, *haus schuhe* my mother would call them, and an electric toothbrush I never use. Tick. Tick. There is it, the travel clock nestled beneath a wash bag. I do not recognise it and it occurs to me that it looks as new as the book. I pull the book out and look at the cover then run my fingers across the raised letters, undulating as low hillocks across a moor. It looks like a memoir with the picture of a woman on the front. My fingertips rise and fall as they would across the weave of the bedspread at home. I am not at home, which is why the tiles are not symmetrical. Where am I, if not there?

I don't remember where home is but I remember the bedspread, and Sandra, a dog and the felt slippers. I usually keep them on my feet or by the bed, and I kick them off only when I write. I am a Writer. I am a Father. I am a Husband. I think Husband should come before Father but it has never felt that way to me. I can hear voices in the corridor again, and see the flicker of white jackets filled with arms and beating chests, clipboards, and hair. Two or three enter the room. Two: An even number.

"Mr Ravenstone, you are still sitting, I see."

"Yes, does it bother you?"

"We told you to rest. Someone can unpack your things."

I am not sure that I want someone to unpack my things.

"I'm fine, thank you. I have everything I need, although some of the items do not look as though they are mine."

"I'm sure your wife packed everything you need."

Wife. It sounds strange to hear the familiar word rolling off the tongue of a stranger in a white coat, as though she were available to anyone. I suppose Sandra is my wife. I suppose it means that I am her husband. Why am I here?

"Thank you," I say, failing to understand why I should be thanking a man in a white jacket.

"Mr Ravenstone, please just lie down."

I open my eyes to find the ceiling straight ahead like a stop sign. I must be lying down now, there is no way forward. I can feel my toes. One. Two. Three. The tiles are still not laid out in an even number. There should be a middle groove where the grouting would lie with four tiles across on either side: four down and eight across all together – thirty two, an even number. The neighbour said something about the lawnmower, about it being unplugged. I always unplug it, always check. And Sandra, she said something about my books. I can't remember what, exactly.

I can hear more footsteps in the corridor: Two, four, six, eight; two less than the length of the corridor, unless it's longer than my count. I pick up the book again, then put it down and wipe the fingerprints from the cover. They ruin the image of the woman's face, mar the sheen. She looks sad. You call tell if someone is sad from the look in their eyes, unless they don't have a look. She has a look – pretty, vulnerable, wanting help, but unable to ask. Not like Sandra, her look is fierce, assertive, self-assured. I like her that way, she doesn't really need me and that is how I like it as long as I can write, and mow the neighbour's lawn, and watch thirty minutes of the news, or twenty five.

I need to get to the sink. The tap is dripping into the white ceramic bowl, echoing into the room in ripples then waves. Everybody has a touch of sadness in them I think, but some are better at hiding behind carnival masks and plastic smiles.

Perhaps there is a way of dealing with sadness without looking as pained as the face on the memoir. The face gives away so much, unless you are a carnival queen who can hide behind layers of colours and feathers. Sandra once said that mine showed nothing. I do not think she meant it exactly. She has a way with words making her sentences sound abrupt, carving through your heart.

The door is still open. It should be shut. There are flashes of white and shoes brushing along the vinyl. Clickety clack, clickety clack. A phone is ringing somewhere in the distance down the corridor. The sound ricochets off the walls and around the corner in to my room. The barrier of white stretches from wall to wall overhead, threatening to close in and crush the life out of my bones. My chest feels tight as though pressured by something. I remember a time when we had to line up at school and we were packed in so tightly that I couldn't breathe.

Sandra is at the door now. I can smell her perfume and feel her presence, her eyes fixed on my body then my bag.

"I packed everything nicely," she said.

"Yes, thank you." I raise my eyebrows and nod.

"Do you like the book?" She looks at the paperback with its undulating letters, resting on the table beside my head. "I thought you'd like it."

"Yes, very kind. She looks sad, don't you think."

I show her the cover. She frowns. I don't know what the frown suggests so I move on.

"How is the dog?"

"Bertie? Yes, he's fine. He misses you."

"How long will I be here? Do you know?"

"It depends on the treatment," she says. "They'll try cognitive therapy to see if it helps to unravel your mind, not that it needs unravelling. All the unfurling happens at your computer. That's why you write, isn't it?" I assume this is a rhetorical question and smile. She grimaces.

"Have I been difficult to live with or unkind in any way?" I ask.

"No, you have just been yourself but the doctor thinks that you need to talk."

"And the ambulance?"

"That was for Mrs Jefferson opposite. She had a heart attack. She's pulling through, though. Don't think about anything except getting better."

Better implies that you are not quite right, or that there could be a problem, or that things are just worse than normal – all phrases my Father used on different occasions, and never in a pleasant way.

"You'll be brighter than moonshine," she says, sounding hopeful. She doesn't always sound hopeful.

"Don't you mean sunshine?" I squint and wait for a response.

"I suppose so, why does it matter? Anyway, you'll be out of here soon. You haven't been yourself since … never mind."

I don't know what she means and I still have an overriding need to wash my hands. I glance at the sink and feel anxious.

"Well, I'm glad they are keeping an eye on you and I'm sure this will help," she says, kissing me on the forehead like a child. She scoops up her shiny bag and walks towards the door without turning back. I hear her footsteps fade as they move towards the exit. She is gone.

I count the tiles again: two, four, six, eight, and I wonder what she meant about me not being myself and I remember, I remember beyond the lawnmower, the dog, and the news. We lost our youngest – our only son – several months ago. I do not remember anything between now and the car crash. I only know that I have felt anxious and my need to count has taken over. It has become all-consuming. I know that they can help, know that they will unravel my mind and stop me from undulating like the shiny words on the book. They will take the sadness from my face and give me a new expression, a glossier one. I know that if they cannot help me here there is nowhere else that can fix things. I take comfort in the fact that I was helping a neighbour and that everything else is all right, and that my wife cared enough to pack my bags and to buy me a book with a face.

I look towards the door and I see clipboards and white then I pick up the book, turn to the first page and read the words. Then I flip back to the cover and see the letters under the face: R.J. Robertson. This is my book. I open the book again, turn to the first page, and begin to read.

Old

Samuel Wright

393 – Clapton – Four minutes. Not bad.

Billy stepped back to his favoured spot behind the bin. He plunged his hands in his pockets. It was by far the best way of dealing with wearing a blazer, but you had to make sure the blazer bunched forward and was tight around your back, otherwise it stuck out behind and revealed your belly at the front and made you look stupid. Under the shelter the girls were already there. Two from the private school, who looked a bit alike only one of them was probably fit and the other one definitely wasn't, and one from the Catholic school who always came to the bus stop with her nan.

The girl and her nan were the main reason he never stood under the shelter, not even when it was raining. He hated them. Well, not hated, but he couldn't be near them. The girl was a weirdo. The uniform for that school was rank anyway, but she was a bit fat and she always wore stockings that only went up to her knees and you could see the tops of them where they bit into her fat knees, and it made her legs look like sausages. The nan was the worst, though. She made his skin crawl. She was just like the girl, only old, and sagged, and just disgusting. She walked like she was a zombie, not a proper zombie, but from those rubbish old films where they couldn't run.

Two minutes. He held on to his Oyster pass in his pocket. He hoped it was just Ryan on the bus. If that other lot were there, Carl, and Joe, and Reece, he'd have to sit with them, but it was quite nice just sitting with Ryan and talking about homework and stuff. And he hoped the Homerton boys weren't there. They once spent a whole journey calling him gay, and he had to just ignore it, and pretend it wasn't happening, because once it happened to Ryan and he said something and they waited until they got off the bus and threw a milkshake at him.

He looked at his watch. 7:33. The Stokie boys were normally on the later one. The drunk guy was circling down by the traffic lights. One minute. People started to shuffle around in the shelter. He walked round the back of it so he'd be in front, ready to flag the bus down. He always flagged the bus down. He knew other people did it too, but he hadn't done it once because he was embarrassed because the fit girl was looking at him, and the bus had just gone past. The bus was approaching. So was the drunk guy. One time, the drunk guy had breathed on him, and it was disgusting, he could smell something rotten inside him. Billy edged nearer the shelter.

The drunk guy got closer. Was he going for the bus? Billy held out his hand to flag the bus down. As it slowed, he backed towards where he predicted it would stop. He mostly got it right. But the drunk guy was going for the bus. Billy backed towards it a little quicker than normal, keeping one eye on the drunk guy.

The bus eased to a stop and Billy turned just as he felt himself bump into something and he put a hand out and pure terror washed over him because he'd backed into the nan and her face was about an inch from his and his hand had pressed into something soft and she made some kind of noise and he could smell her and he went "Sorry!" and stepped back and he felt the sweat start under his arms and he felt sick because he was sure that was her tit. He'd touched her tit.

They trooped on to the bus. His Oyster beeped. He went for the stairs. All he could think of was her tit. The feel of her tit. It was gross, like a deflated balloon. It was soft. Too soft. And her face. He'd been so close to her face that he couldn't even pretend it hadn't happened. Her face was so sagged and fat, her tit must be like that too. Her mouth was the worst. It was like it had melted a bit, so that the hole was lower than normal people and instead of seeing two sets of teeth, above and below, you just saw the bottom half of the lower teeth and a horrible grey lumpy bit of gum. It was like she had no strength in her lips to close her mouth, and the bottom one just flapped open, a useless bit of flesh.

"Billy!"

He blinked. It was Reece. He was sat with Carl and Joe. They each were spread across a double seat and there was one spare on the other side of the aisle. Ryan was sitting four rows beyond them, near the back. Billy sat down.

"Nah, there was bare gash. It was sick, bruv, honestly."

Carl was talking to Joe. His face was bright and he was doing that jerky thing, where he looked like he was having an electric shock. Billy only ever saw him on the bus because most of the time in school he was in special needs. "Even that wasteman, what's his name, that one with glasses, even he was lipsing some Year 7."

Billy knew they must be talking about the fireworks in Victoria Park. He'd gone with his Dad, but he knew everyone else went on their own and met up with the Clapton girls.

"I heard Liban got off with Johnny Palmer's sister," said Joe slowly. He always spoke slowly, as if he was thinking over every word.

"Matthew saw him. He said he touched her tits."

Billy saw his opening.

"Nah, bruv, don't even talk about it." He shook his head solemnly.

"What?"

"Tits, bruv. Man, that was awful."

"What?"

Billy leant in, his face animated. He spoke in a piercing whisper. "Man, I just touched some granny's tit by mistake in the queue!"

"Urhh!"

All of them burst out into cackles of laughter.

"It was bare rank! And her face! She was proper rank! It was like her face had fallen off!"

"Urhh!"

Billy felt a thrill of excitement. They were properly laughing. It was great when you said something and they all laughed. There was always a risk, though. Sometimes someone might use it against you, no matter what it was. He'd got torn apart a few weeks back for saying he'd fingered Latitia, when he'd thought it was probably the coolest thing he'd ever done.

Carl's face suddenly fell serious. "Oh, no, I tell you what, though, did you see that thing last night? That monkey thing?"

"Yeah!" Reece's face was a mask of delighted horror.

"That was bare disgusting!"

"Nah, honestly, I was going to be sick, bruv," Carl said.

"I was going to vomit."

"What monkey thing?" said Billy.

"Didn't you see it?"

"What?"

"Oprah. It's in the papers. Some lady got her face ripped off by a monkey."

"Oh my days!"

"She got her face ripped off, her whole face, like there was nothing left, and her hands ripped off too."

"Oh my days!"

They sat in stunned and appreciative silence for a moment. That was pretty extreme, Billy thought. That was like in *Silence of the Lambs*. He wished he'd seen it. He'd watched *Silence of the Lambs* a few months back, and he thought it was the best film he'd ever seen. He remembered the bit where the guy got his face bitten off, and you just saw his teeth without lips. He thought with an odd queasiness about the nan's face.

Joe was gearing up to say something. He looked thoughtful. "But she got, like, thirty million pounds compensation."

Reece was intrigued. "Really?"

Joe carried on. "Yeah, she got thirty million pounds. And she was on Oprah."

"Thirty million pounds, just for getting her face ripped off by a monkey?" said Reece.

"Yeah, but it's pretty bad, though," said Billy.

"Yeah, but, like, thirty million pounds!"

"Would you do it?" said Carl.

Everyone was silent for a moment. Then Joe spelt it out. "What, get your face and hands ripped off by a monkey for thirty million pounds?"

Carl nodded. "Yeah."

Joe thought carefully. Billy could see that everyone else was thinking too. He didn't really want to imagine it. He felt a bit uncomfortable.

He looked around. The bus was pretty full now. He saw, with a sudden lurch in his gut, the girl and her nan sat three rows in front. They sat with the same hunch in their shoulders. The nan was in the window seat. She was facing out. He could see her profile. Her eyes sagged just like her mouth and they seemed all of a sudden like the saddest things he had ever seen.

"I'd do it," said Joe. "You could buy a flat screen TV."

Carl jeered at him. "What! That's bare stupid. You've got no eyes, bruv, your whole face is ripped off. You don't even have no hands to change channels!"

They all began jeering too. Joe struggled against the noise to say "I don't care, I'd do it!"

Billy was silent. The noise was sharp and brutal. He looked at Carl's crazy little face, all twisted and laughing. He felt an odd lightness. His hand rested on the bus seat, and he felt the fabric under it. The sun glinted on the windows of the parked cars they passed, and the bus engine chuntered and roared. He lifted a hand to touch his face, and imagined it old.

13

Howard Cunnell

Cherry kicked at empty bottles and cans on the blackened ground, a partly melted lime-green plastic lighter, pieces of browned foil. Sunlight came to her through the stand of birch trees in a fractured cascade. She could feel the ground's heat through her boots. She was hydrous, boneless, all sweat and loss. Dad kept saying he'd never known a summer in London this hot. The grass in the park was yellow and dead and the trees were tinder-dry.

Cherry wiped her wet face, picked up her canvas bag from where she'd thrown it on the ground, and found her water bottle. There wasn't much left. She drank just enough to wet her mouth. The water was warm and tasted like it had been closed in too long.

Sweat blurred her vision and fell thick as honey to the ground. A crow on a high treetop was a crow-shaped black hole in the sky. She wiped her face again and felt in her bag for the cigarette she'd taken from her brother's room. She lit it with one of the three lime-green lighters she had in her cut-off pockets. Brother. The word still sounded weird but she had to stop thinking of Jay as a girl.

"I hate being mispronounced," Jay had said to her. "Imagine if somebody called you 'he'."

His black hair chopped down, his right arm a red mess of scars. Cherry didn't know if Jay's voice sounded deep because he practiced or because of the tight binders he wore to flatten his breasts.

"Yeah," Cherry had said, because she couldn't help herself, "but I *am* a girl. Oww! Jay! Fuck off! I was joking!"

She felt more African than usual.

There was something about the sunlight coming broken through the trees that suggested the bright kente cloth her mother wore as she sang in her grandfather's red-dirt compound in Accra, on a Sunday morning before church.

Maybe it was the drugs she was taking. 10mg of Escitalopram every day, and Diazepam for whenever she needed it. Whatever was in the pills gave her vivid dreams that bled into the day.

I'll be 14 tomorrow. What will that be like?

Cherry had kept most of her toys from when she was little. A soft blue octopus she'd thrown a screaming tantrum to get when she was tiny. A tatty hammerhead shark Dad had brought back from one of his trips years ago. A strawberry and vanilla-coloured Polly Pocket plane that opened at the roof so you could put all the tiny people inside, and sit them on their tiny seats, and that for some reason made her think of planes exploding, falling out of the sky.

The octopus and the ragged shark slept in her bed. The now wingless plane was on a cluttered shelf, upside down, its sides folded open and exposing the insides. The little people were scattered on the shelf – some of them had arms or legs missing, and there was one with a melted face after Cherry had burnt him.

In a drawer she kept pictures of Jay when he was still her sister. Jay had made her take them off the wall.

Her phone rang. Oh my gosh it was hot.

Jay had said that smoking helped stress but Cherry just felt sick. She sifted through the rubbish with a stick but there wasn't much left to burn. The strange white ash looked solid until she poked it. A kind of fine powder was briefly visible on the air and then it disappeared.

Jay was such a shithead and he used everyone. He was spending the summer at a camp with other trans kids.

She held the end of the cigarette to a wafer of black bark. The bark's incandescent rim became the remembered blood-orange sun of her childhood visits to Africa, falling beyond Accra's dark horizon.

Her phone rang again.

She was supposed to be at the pool with Dad. It was a big deal. He'd wanted them to have a swim together on his last day.

This morning he'd have gone into her room before work and see she hadn't been home. See her wet swimsuit and towel on the floor where she'd left them. Every time he went into her room he'd say, "How can you live in a tip like this Cher?"

He was such a grumpy prick.

Last night she'd heard Mum talking about the end of the season at the pool and asking Dad what he was going to do for work now.

"We've spent all the money sending Jay to camp," Mum had said.

"I'll find work," Dad had said.

"You should have sorted something out already," Mum had said, "You knew the pool was closing. Don't walk away when I'm talking. Where are you going?"

Later she heard other voices – Dad's friends, men he had brought back from the pub. Cherry heard the men talking loudly about the kids – everybody said it was kids – who were out setting fires in the park at night. She had got out the house soon after. Mum and Dad would forget to kiss her goodnight as usual so she was safe.

Dad's arms were filled with lucky charm tattoos – and when she was really small he'd say, "Cher, find the little fish, find the anchor, find the red flower Cher. Tell me something I don't know. What did you find out today?" Huffing close to her ear. "Let me smell your head."

Kissing her neck, blowing a raspberry. His smells she could name now – tobacco, chlorine, beer and after-sun. Her tiny brown fingers tracing her Dad's tattoos, adding new, invisible patterns to those already on his warm skin. Sometimes he let her use felt-tips to colour in the small spaces on his arms that weren't tattooed. He would curl her hair round his finger while she worked. Now he hardly seemed to notice her when she walked into a room.

Cherry watched the light-skinned boy coming from the direction of the dried out pond. She could hear cans of drink moving against each other in the blue plastic bag he carried, the blue an unreal colour in the sun-bleached landscape.

The boy's rough Afro was tied back and he was shirtless. Cherry recognised him but she didn't know his name. She'd never seen him on his own before.

Grasshoppers sawed in the dead grass. It was otherwise still and quiet under the trees and she could hear the boy panting when he sat down next to her. There were hands in prayer and holding a rosary tattooed on his neck, and underneath was printed *Only God Can Judge Me*.

"I know you," he said, "what are you doing here? Why aren't you at the pool?"

"Why should I be?"

"Everybody else is."

"Why aren't you then?"

"I've been there already," the light-skinned boy said. He looked at her. "But you like it in there, I know you do. So why aren't you there?"

Cherry shrugged.

The boy gazed at the sweat pooling on his hairless chest.

"It is hot though," he said. "You look hot. Why ain't you down there?"

"Where are your friends?" Cherry said.

"Where are yours?"

Cherry shook her dark head.

"My brother steals all my friends," she said.

A grey heron rose vertically in the pale sky. They watched without speaking until the bird disappeared.

"My Dad's down there," the boy said.

"In the pool?"

"Yeah."

"Are you supposed to be with him?"

"You like being mixed-race?" he said.

"It's all right."

"Too black for white, too white for black," he said.

"Everybody thinks I'm Hispanic," she said, "it's so annoying."

"Does your Dad care where you are?" the boy said.

Cherry shrugged again.

"Why are you out here by yourself?"

Cherry poked at the blackened ground.

"Did you do this?" the boy said.

She flicked the lighter on and waved the flame at him.

"Can I have a drink?"

The boy pulled a can of Raspberry Colt Blast out of the bag. He felt it. "Warm," he said, and stood up.

"Come on." He put his hand out. Cherry let him pull her up.

"Where are we going?" she said.

"Nowhere. Come on."

They started to walk.

"Dog," the boy said.

"What?"

"Through there. See him?"

The white dog jogged slowly across the park.

"Is he all right?" Cherry said, "He's all alone."

"He's all right."

The dog pitched on his back, kicking and rolling on the ground, raising a scrim of veiling dust.

"See?" The boy said. His eyes were shining.

What was it about men and their dogs? A couple of times that summer, she'd let Dad drag her along on the dawn walks he took in the park with his friends and their dogs. The only time it was cool enough for the dogs to run, Dad had said.

The way these men talked to their dogs! The cooing and baby talk that went on.

They walked across the park, away from the blackened ground. Through Cherry's cut-off jeans pocket the three lighters were warm against her skin. They came to a rise where she could look down to the valley of the park and the impossible brightness of the pool. Her Dad had been taking her there forever. Her phone rang and rang. The boy looked at her. Under his pretty curled lashes his green eyes were shaped like sunflower seeds or little fishes so that she thought he might be part Chinese. Sweat popped on his skin.

"Why don't you turn it off if you're not going to answer it?" he said.

The blue water of the pool seemed a long way away.

"My Dad's in charge down there," she said. "At least he is until tomorrow. Some leisure company's going to turn it into a gym. Dad says people like us won't be able to go there anymore."

The live oak was so large it was like its own forest, with high branches that were as big as any two other trees put together.

They sat on opposite sides. The huge, corrugated plates of bark were cool against her back. She thought she could hear air moving around inside the tree. Was it hollow?

She turned her head to press her ear against the bark, and so she missed some of what the boy said, but he told her his name was Justin, and that he lived on the Stockwell Park Estate with his Mum and his baby half-sister Mahera. Justin said his Dad sold weed out of a room in the Barrier Block on Coldharbour Lane.

Justin's voice tuned in and out of different frequencies. Radio Tough and the Bullshit Station. She heard cute fading into lonely.

The branches were black rivers cut into the sky.

"This tree's over six hundred years old," she said.

"That's nothing," Justin said, "I've seen older ones."

"Where?"

"In my Dad's yard."

"This tree knows when you're lying Justin."

She heard him get up. She counted nine before he reached her side of the tree. He sat down, and then kind of slowly fell into her until his head was in her lap. Cherry stared at the hands in prayer tattooed on Justin's neck.

"Is your little sister cute?" she said.

"Mahera rides on my back," Justin said. "She calls me 'Stin cos she can't say Justin."

"Mum says there's no such thing as half-sisters or brothers."

"My Mum likes Mahera 'cos she's brand new," Justin said. "And she's a girl. When I'm there I feel like a dirty ghost. I'd rather stay with my Dad, but I don't go there too much."

"Why not?"

"He tells me it's not safe but really he doesn't want me there. When he's drunk he'll say things like, boy you are always in my way. Like a joke but I know he means it for real."

"They used to put witches up against this tree and leave them to live or die," Cherry said.

"Witches? Girl, I know it's you lying to me now."

"It's true, my Mum told me."

"How they know who was a witch?"

"If they thought you were a witch they'd tie you to the tree with ropes. If you died that proved you weren't a witch, but if you didn't it proved you were. They burnt the ones who lived."

"That's fucked up," Justin said. "Are you a witch?"

"My brother might be."

"How's a boy a witch?"

So she told Justin all about Jay. How Jay had once been a girl and was now a boy. The way Jay told it, he'd always been a boy but in a girl's body.

"It's not bad all the time," Jay had said, "I have fun, too."

"Fun times," Cherry had said.

"Yeah, you know, when I'm not thinking about this stuff all the time. Then somebody calls me a girl and all I can think about is how everything in here is a boy but there's all this shit hanging off me."

Justin smoked a joint while she talked. He offered it to Cherry and she shook her head, reaching down to pick burnt dead grass from his long hair.

"I don't," she said, interrupting her story.

Justin looked at her, his eyes widening.

"I know," she said, "it's like I'm the only one. My Dad, my Mum. They all smoke."

Justin smoked, and lay on his side not looking at her, burning insects.

"Don't do that," Cherry said.

"Why not?"

"How would you like it?"

Justin laughed and burnt some more ants. He jabbed at a lacewing but it flew away, its transparent wings whirring slowly through the shimmering heat wave.

The tattoo was like a three dimensional growth coming out of Justin's neck. Cherry could almost believe that the hands had been grafted on, and Justin was hosting them for a friend, even maybe for his little sister, Mahera, who Cherry suddenly imagined being born without hands.

She told her story and her stupid thoughts moved behind her eyes in an unstoppable ribbon of pictures and words. An extra pair of hands. Give me a hand.

She counted fourteen crows that weren't moving.

Justin smoked.

"So your sister's going to get her tits cut off and have a dick stuck on," he said. "And then she'll be your brother? Ain't nobody going to do that to Mahera."

A boy with hands in prayer and *Only God Can Judge Me* tattooed on his neck.

Cherry knew the next line of the song: *All you other motherfuckers get out of my business.*

Postcards from Paradise

Trine V. Ipsen

She kept his postcards in the special shoebox, the one with "Treasures" written on the top in her best cursive handwriting. It was framed with glitter-hearts and the puffy stickers of birds and butterflies he gave her for her ninth birthday two months ago. The latest postcard showed a city of skyscrapers right by the beach, almost tipping into the turquoise ocean; older cards had koala bears and kangaroos on the shiny paper. She liked the one where the world map was upside down. "Because you are on top of the world" he had written with a blue pen across the card with an arrow pointing to New Zealand and a smiling stick figure girl on top of the islands.

The plane from Auckland landed at 1.35pm in the Gold Coast airport. Her father's face lit up when he spotted her walking out from the baggage area. "How grown up you are," he said in disbelief while holding her tight into his chest. He smelled like Dad; wood, smoke and something sharp and too familiar. She breathed through her mouth and enjoyed having him right here with her.

"You are so brown," she said to him in the car.

He grinned. "And you're so pale. Let's change that and go to the beach. What do you say?"

"Now? I need to call Mom."

"No worries. You can call her from the beach. You've got your swimsuit in your suitcase, don't you? I have towels in the back. Don't look like that. You can sleep soon enough. Besides, what better place is there to lie down than on the sand?"

She became red instead of brown and the ocean was more dark blue than light turquoise, but she still thought it was the greatest place on the planet; palm trees and colourful parrots complaining about nothing. The water woke every inch of her body from her little toes to her heavy head. Refreshed, she wrestled with the Pacific Ocean.

When she got out to rest, her father gave her a pineapple juice and he himself was drinking from the tartan patterned thermos she recognised right away. There had never been tea or coffee in it. She drank her juice quickly, and though she did not have the energy for another round with the waves, she ran back into the blue anyway. By the time she returned, he had emptied the thermos. She lay down beside him, making sure he blocked her view of that tartan pattern.

He let her decide dinner and they had burgers and milkshakes on the balcony while the sunset turned the sky into a rainbow. The apartment faced away from the ocean towards the other resorts of Main Beach; when darkness came, the lit windows of the dispersed towers made Catherine feel like she was floating in a huge coral reef.

"You could stay if you wanted to," he suggested over breakfast. "For a year maybe. It would only be fair since you've been with your mother for a year now."

"Stay here at the beach with you?" she asked, surprised.

"I'm looking for another place in the city so it wouldn't be here exactly, but nowhere is too far from the beach on the Gold Coast," he assured her. "Think about it."

He gave her a key before they left and she got to lock the door. "This should be your home as much as your mother's is. You're my Paradise Girl," he said and kissed her on top of the head.

Another glorious day at the beach; another emptied thermos. For dinner they had lasagne and he had a beer, though she had wanted milkshakes again. "What would your mother say if I let you have milkshakes every night?" Catherine would have answered that she wanted the milkshakes so he would have had something nice to drink that was not beer, but she had tried that when he still lived with them back home and he had not responded well.

He let her pick a movie and put it on.

"I'm going down to see a couple of mates, okay? Are you good here with the movie?"

When the movie finished she went straight to sleep. She did not want to be awake when he came home and hear those unsteady steps, worrying if he would keep his balance.

They walked to Surfers Paradise along the beach, talking about how she would come here to live with him; everyday a summer's day. There were too many cars by day, too many flying foxes by night and the buildings somehow reminded her of old eggshells, but the beach made up for all the city's roughness and strangeness. The beach was where her dreams lived; dreams of koalas and kangaroos and endless days in the sand with her dad.

"Pick us a couple of lollies," he said after lunch. She picked out two light blue ones with blueberry flavour. They walked back towards the beach and passed a pub on the way. The water was right there in front of them when he stopped.

"You know what, I think I saw my mate in one of the places we passed by. Would you mind meeting up at the beach in a moment? I just have to say hello. Won't be long."

She held the two lollies, one in each hand, and sat on the sand waiting. The sky was clear and the sun shone through the frozen lollies; it did not take them long to start melting. She was going to enjoy her lolly when he came back which would not be long. She watched while the sugar-water ran down to cool her warm hands and drip to the sand. He was going to be here in a moment. The lollies lost their sharp shape. He would come. More of the lollies had melted onto the sand now than remained on the wooden sticks. She did not leave the beach until the lollies had completely melted.

They did not talk when he got home around eight that night. She pretended to be asleep and he pretended to believe it. The next day he took her to Sea World and bought her a dolphin teddy. They talked and smiled, but not about her staying on the Gold Coast or him forgetting her on the beach. When she boarded the flight home at the end of the week, they both knew she would not return to Paradise.

To Become Immortal

Seth Clabough

1

You'll want to grow up in a loveless house and lose your two best childhood friends. Chakana will need to go first. The last time you'll see him is for coffee outside City Bistro on the downtown mall. A year from now this will be last February and you'll remember him lounging there with his eyes the colour of an avocado nut, his long arms resting on the chair back and him saying something like "the transitory nature of *everything* makes current conditions irrelevant" and then up and drowning over spring break, on the coast of Limón, in a plastic baby pool.

Celia-Rose – with her red lips orange hair, and jittery hands – will need to go next. Probably in the basement with her stepfather's .22 target pistol, the only item bequeathed to him by a grandmother who, after selling the last of her furniture, said "Nothing is forever" and then let her legs swell up and go purple before dying in a Sarasotan DNR care facility.

As to the visions – the dead with their blue lips, creatures lurking beneath the ice in the deep oceans on Europa, Andromeda cannibalising the Milky Way – these are far less important than thinking of Earth as an inert sphere of metal, rock, and gas arranged in layers. Avoid, at all costs, realising it's not inert, that it's a whole intertwined system of spheres (*atmo, litho, hydro*), that it takes a continuously operating machine to harbour lives such as these.

2

Next, at the funeral of a distant relative, you'll need to be embraced by a big woman in a floral dress, with circular sunglasses and a wide-brimmed hat. In her eyes you'll see the renegade comets of the Oort Cloud. Ignore them.

"Don't worry, dear," she'll say with her lips to your ear as people file out of the church. "It's not like someone's targeting your friends and family, is it?" You'll know it's her because she'll smell faintly of kitty litter and creeping thyme and because when you don't see her at the graveside service no one you ask will remember such a lady.

After that you'll rent an apartment in the city. Let a year pass and then another. Wear your father's fedora. Fail at your relationships. Go out for drinks with friends you hate. Watch them plummet into marriage, gain weight, and post pictures of their ugly kids. Unfriend them. Go out for drinks alone. On the New Year's Eve following your parents' murder-suicide, get drunk on White Russians while playing nine-ball at Miller's and go home with a car salesman named Dennis. Throw up from balconies. Make appointments with realtors, but don't show up; develop a sense of irony, then dial the out-of-service numbers of childhood friends.

What will happen next is this: you'll be eating eggs benedict at *Mono Loco*. Make sure it's Sunday, that you're sitting outside, that nobody loves you, that the edges of the sky are burnt orange. That's when it will happen. If the conditions are right, you'll feel that pustule of bother move in your gut.

3

From there the final steps are easy: break your lease, leave everything behind and use your inheritance to buy a cattle farm with a pond in Appomattox. There will likely be an old double-wide on the property. Move into it. Since neutrinos are passing through your body, through entire planets untouched, no one will blame you for ignoring cows. Nourish that pustule, coax it along with regret and insomnia.

Collect trinkets and do-dads via the internet from distant countries. Buy lots of *stuff* and stack it unopened. Become a hoarder. Tell yourself only Celia-Rose and Chakana could understand. Cut the fences and let the cattle roam, let your dreams be plagued by a fat woman in a big hat. She'll want to sit on your chest, force kitty litter down your throat, hold your mouth shut and pinch your nose. Let her. It's like this: because your mother was gay, because she cried at the sink with her back to everyone – tears smaller than a ladybug's wing – because she was in love with a planetarium guide named Maxine, because your father once said "misery is a city with more roads leading to it than people to visit" and really meant it, because they aged to become exaggerated versions of their own worst parts.

But you're above all that now. Even death – theirs, yours, the friends you hate. All that worries you are the peripheries: Celia-Rose surrounded in that basement at her passing not by loved ones, but the odds and ends of her mother's failed nostalgia shop – Danish salt and pepper shakers, mouldy Raggedy Anne and Andy dolls, how they found her on a replica of a tapestry purportedly woven in Brussels, during the middle ages, for Charles V. What bothers you is knowing how *cola de chancho fritas* floated in the little pool with Chakana, how the only other attendees at his drowning were a crumpled pack of Galouises, a decorative Sarchi oxcart, and the faded photo of a seventh grade girl who years ago had moved away. Sure it's depressing, but what this will show you is liberating: it's the details that open portals for death to crawl out.

4

Once you've acquired and jailed in unopened boxes all the little details you can and once the doublewide is too full of those items to get to the bathroom or kitchen, it's finally time to travel to Lynnhaven Used Boats in Portsmith and buy an old trailerable Aqua Casa 16. Get the blue one with the missing seat cushions. Have them deliver it. No matter how they look at you, insist that they put it in the pond.

Take up smoking, if you want. Menthols. Sit on the poop deck and swill warm malt liquor from a tin cup. Who needs friends or parents – any models of happiness to follow – when you have a houseboat, Wi-Fi, instant coffee. Do buy a cockatiel, but store everything on the tiny dock. The boat must be clean and bare at all times. Watch the signalling of afternoon light on the water, the flashing of it on the twisting aluminium foil surface. Ignore the handful of malnourished cows that haven't wandered off, that come to lower their mouths to the pond and glower at you and your little floating kingdom. Tell yourself you never wanted to marry anyway, that you can't be fooled by pain anymore, that you know how it's for its own benefit, how it's like the way fire will burn everything it can, how it wants more of the stuff that keeps it going, that keeps it alive.

Rub your stomach. Name your bother and wait for it to emerge. A bother changes everything. The sun rises and sets. Years will want to pass. Let them. It's up to other people now to worry about why the songs of children still linger over burned down houses.

5

The last part is fairly simple: Float in your circlet. Bump gently (and frequently) against the shore. Reach for items on the dock as you drift by. It's like an orbit, if you think about it. And if you concentrate, you can feel the moon's gravity pulling at the edges of the pond. You can eat when you want but don't sleep too often – you have your little bother to think about. Peer through the windows to check the seals on the boxes in the doublewide. The purchases want out, after all. They want to populate your background, to become peripheries, to open a portal big enough for a fat lady in a wide hat.

Sure, it's frightening, but you can prevent it now. Wave to the items on the dock – the coffee, tin cup, the cigarettes, the despondent cockatiel. There's nothing around you. Bask in that power, in your resulting immortality, in the fact that you can remember, without feeling, the day your mother took you to the planetarium. How, when she thought you were watching the light show, you were really watching the guide hold your mother's hand in the dark. How, when Maxine said, "Whole galaxies are moving away from us at ever increasing speeds, Lucy, some so far out they'll soon be gone forever," your mother said, "I know, but forever still has to do with time. And what's forever compared to this?" and then turned to hide her tears.

Tonight, though, there are no stars visible above the Aqua Casa, and it's happened. You're finally holding your little bother in your arms. The gestation was so long, but now you can touch it, kiss it, get to know it. You have nothing but centuries ahead. You have forever. It's amazing, isn't it? How such a tiny thing can shrink the world, how there are no connections, how nothing *really can be* forever.

Prey

Michelle Wright

The afternoon warmth has drifted away so she rolls her sleeves down over her wrists. It was a good idea to stay on at the library after class. Got it all done and leaves her free. An evening of stillness and peace. As she crosses the train station car park, she starts at a flapping of wings. A crow scrabbles on the slick surface of a car bonnet, eating a hardened crust of bread. Raps it against the metal till it breaks into beak-sized pieces. She looks away from its chalk-white eyes and takes out her keys. Another week till her dad comes home. She cherishes the independence, eating what she likes, walking around the house naked. She might call Sean tonight. Thinks she might like to see him.

As she hits the car park asphalt the air is punched out of her lungs, and before she can take a full breath in he's on top and has pinned her down. His knee pressed so hard on her back that she can't even gasp. And even when he pulls down her underpants and rapes her with his fingers from behind, all she can think is: *air … air … air.*

It's over in a minute, as she'll tell the policewoman later, though it might have been two or three. When she hears him running off, she opens her eyes and sees the bright yellow soles of his sneakers flash away. She lies where she fell, not able to move. Her arms are wrung out towels and the brain signals jolt and sputter. The cold of the ground has turned her lips blue, or maybe it's the shock, and her scalp pricks and tightens. She breathes deep through her nose. *Asphalt smells like petrol when your face is up this close. Who else has smelt this smell?* she wonders. *Who else has been down here?* Her right arm is pinned under her, but she pulls it free and brings it to her face. She pushes a tuft of tomato-red hair away from her eyes and asks *What's that?* as the streetlight glints on something not far from her cheek. This close up it looks like a diamond. She heaves up onto her knees and sees it's a shattered beer bottle that's been lying in wait for unprotected flesh.

He'd pressed so hard that the doctors have to cut deep to take out the crumbled jags of glass embedded in her cheek and chin, and one in the front of her shoulder. They say the scars will be small, but she knows they'll be all she'll see in every reflection she glimpses walking past a window or a mirror. The nurses worry she's taking a taxi home. *There's no one can stay with you tonight?* they ask. She'll be fine, she assures them, feeling sick, not wanting to picture telling her dad.

In the laundry she stuffs her skirt and underwear into the poppy-covered tote bag. She'd bought it at the market just last week. She'd been so pleased to find it. She opens the laundry door and buries it all down in the bottom of the wheelie bin.

Under the shower the water pricks then soothes and she simply lets it flow. The bathroom fan has broken, so when she turns off the taps there's an un-normal silence without the rattling cover. She steps out of the shower as if into a cloud, lulled and breathing thin. She dabs her skin dry and puts on fresh pyjamas.

So many doors to check in the house. Windows and doors to cover and lock. Her bedroom window so low to the ground; so easy to break and step right in. She takes an hour to drag the wardrobe in front of it. After, her arms and legs tremble and sweat with the effort. It's easier to move the television cabinet in front of the wide bay window, and then all that's left is to double check the laundry door.

Sitting on an armchair in the silence of the lounge room, she calls her sister. *Hey, leave a message* is all she gets. The cat is on edge and won't come near her. She picks it up and puts it on her lap, but it takes off, digging its claws into her thighs and leaving rows of red dots behind that soak up through the cotton and stain her white pyjamas.

As the light begins to fade, she gets up to adjust the curtain. The cat has brushed against it and there's a slit of window showing. She lies flat on the carpet and slides towards the wall. The cat jumps up on the couch and watches, its whiskers twitching. With two fingers, she takes hold of the bottom of the curtain and gently moves it to the right. Not a brusque movement. Just slowly closes the gap. Then she slides and backs away till her shadow's out of sight and pulls herself back up on the armchair. She takes a long sip from her drink and the cat pauses, watches, waits. "Stop staring!" she snarls and hides behind her mug.

The clicks and coos increase as the night slips on. From one to two in the morning she sleeps, not meaning to. She wakes, angry at herself, her jaw sore from clenching. She chain-drinks coffee till four, willing the sun to rise. The darkness is crushing and she wishes for the day, but she can't speak it into existence and she can't chance turning on a light. Like wartime blackouts. Just a chink of light between the curtains can give it all away.

Her life has gone into black and white, but when she looks in the mirror her flame-red hair is on fire and it's saying: *Here I am ... it's me ... I'm the one.* She feels so visible, so easy to spot. To find again and finish off.

To make the trip to the shops, she takes precautions and covers herself. An old grey parka with a hood, with her hair tucked right in and her mother's huge round Jackie O sunglasses. The supermarket opens at six, so she sets off at five forty-five. She scurries from doorway to doorway, to limit her exposure, like a grey mouse with its bulging eyes. The old rational part of her brain can see she's being crazy, but the new connections are strengthening with every crazy thought and she's losing the will to be anything else.

In the beauty aisle she spends too long choosing, knowing she's standing out. She keeps her eyes down, scanning the shoes. Sneakers hustle past and skirt her – white soles, blue, orange, green. Finally she finds the right hair-dye: a blend-in brown – the dullest shade – like her dad's overcooked roast beef.

The sky is light caramel when she arrives back in her yard. A shadow flows across the lawn and ripples over her skin. She follows it as it slips over the neighbour's fence. From a tall tree next door – *Has it always been so tall?* – a massive bird of prey observes its realm. She opens her mouth and thinks: *Since when do you live here? I've not seen you before?*

She goes inside and straight to the bathroom. The instructions say thirty minutes, but it'll take longer to cover her last *Electric Lava* dye job. She sits on the edge of the bath and counts, dye seeping down her neck and colouring her temples. When she washes it out, the water runs brown like dirty dishwashing scum.

She dries her hair and curls up on her dad's bed, closing her eyes to rest. When she wakes the day is gone and over. Her head is light with hunger and walking down the hallway, she skims against the walls. In the lounge room she stops and hears a cat outside. It belongs to one of the neighbours, or did. Now it just roams the yards, pacing back and forth, whining by the front door, sniffing for food or females. She looks out through the peephole and spies it on the lawn, turning its ears and licking at a dead mouse held down in its claw. Still positioned in the tree, the bird of prey peers down. Its dark brown feathers shiver in the breeze. The cat continues. No idea it's being watched. It pulls at the mouse, detaching some flesh and lifts its head to swallow. As it lowers its neck to continue, the bird springs off from the branch. Light and fluid like a diver from the ten metre board, but with not a twinge of self-doubt. It swoops, its wings held tight against its body, stocky legs tucked under its tail. It doesn't screech or squawk, doesn't make a sound. Just the whistle of the air, or is that in her head? In the short distance from the tree to the lawn, it works up a startling speed. Before it hits, its wings swivel and brake and it extends its talons forward like a jumbo jet coming in to land.

The cat is pinned down by the neck and one leg and it screams – more in protest than in pain. The bird thrashes and scuffles to firm the grasp of its claws. Its head curves down, and the sun catches a copper ruffle on its neck. Wings and legs – brown and black – flap wildly, and feathers and fur come out at the roots. The cat turns its head searching for a target. The bird jumps and the cat is flipped onto its back. It hisses at its attacker's chest, but the big bird manoeuvres its talons to keep the teeth at bay. The bird's beak hooks and tears and flesh comes free. Fur, blood and sinews fly and land, and long pink strands are pulled. And then with one deep wing beat, it's off. No change in its expression, just the self-possessed frown of another job done.

When it disappears behind the neighbour's roof, she unlocks the door and steps out onto the landing. The death scene is deserted and fur blows in the breeze and catches on the rosebush thorns. The half-eaten mouse is still on the lawn. Above the trees the bird reappears without its catch. It must have dropped it or stowed it safely. *Where would it stow it?* she wonders. The bird climbs then banks, then climbs still higher, till the earth flattens out, making a map of homes and parks and people.

And she, with her blend-in hair, is a well-camouflaged form far below against the brown wooden planks of the landing. The bird glides and circles, taking it all in. Just the fluttering of air through the tips of its wings, it scans its domain. Lined basketball courts where schoolyard scraps blow up against the cyclone fence. Fleshy children's fingers wrapped around the monkey bars where she used to swing. The tree-shadowed creek, where ducks drift downstream like drowsy commuters on the six a.m train, leaving silver arrows in their wake.

The bird circles and climbs and dips its beak to look down again, and she follows it from way below. On the main street, the soft trace of a chalk Renoir is fading, scuffed bare by passing feet. A policeman gives directions to a man on a bike with a rainbow-coloured parasol attached. The bare liver-spotted scalp of the bag man on the bench she'd carved her name on one cold afternoon. The bird banks and takes in the glint of broken glass still lying in wait in the car park and the slick car bonnets parked nearby. It circles once more, and looks with pity on the tops of the cowered heads of all the careful people hastening home as darkness falls. She strains her neck to see it still. It is climbing higher now, moving out of human scope. She feels a tremor in her chest that tells her to stand there and wait. For the stillness to settle in and for the light to die away.

Schwellenangst

Jeremy Tiang

She can just make out the words in the fading sunlight: "The only good system is a sound system." The concrete façade is marred in patches, but several stretches are still pristine grey, damaged only by the salt air and bird droppings – the vandals defeated by its sheer length. Most of the graffiti is in German, but language here is no badge of authenticity. Everyone Joy has met seems eager to parade their English before her. Even the older residents, the ones who learnt Russian at school, pepper their dialogue with it. "Auf meinem To-do List stehen drei Urgent Emails."

Her own German is rusty, but fine for ordinary conversation. She isn't bothered about details like gender. It makes no sense, anyway, that 'sea' is feminine but 'ocean' neutral. She tries both out, looking at the glittering water just visible through a screen of pine trees. "Das Meer. Die Ostsee." The Baltic, starting here on the Northern German coast and rising in a silver arc along the Scandinavian peninsula.

She has been walking for almost an hour, yet there is no sign the building will surprise her. Its uniformity is strength, the sheer brute force of a monolithic bulwark against – what? On the way over, when they stopped for lunch, the fat woman who ran the café tried to talk them out of staying there. "Go to Binz instead," she insisted. "Nicer there. Not so much history."

Joy tried to explain that history was exactly what they were after, why the school was sending twenty-three of its brightest A-Level candidates on a journey away from anything normal teenagers might find exciting. The Head of Department having decided the way to truly understand a language is to know the past of its speakers, they have gone in search of artefacts.

And now, Prora. They arrived that afternoon, but the real exploration will take place tomorrow. Her solo walk around is ostensibly to identify potential problems in their route, but really she wants to experience the building without the distraction of two dozen well-meaning but unbiddable young people. The daytrippers have long gone, and she has the narrow footpath to herself.

Even with the wind, she can hear vague throbbing that resolves into a bass line as she nears a row of broken windows with light behind them. Not the steady glow of normal lamps, but flickers and flashes. Torches? Then she gets closer and it is obvious. As she watches, a tallish red-haired man steps from a window, finding his footing on the ledge, lighting a cigarette. They eye each other. She calls up, Englishly polite even when speaking another language, "Entschuldigung, ist hier einen Rave?" Hoping the German word is the same as in English, as they so often are.

He shrugs. "Name it what you like." His English is excellent, with only a trace of accent. "Come up, come in, if you like. Why not?"

There are many reasons why not, but she finds herself testing the first step of the ladder, gripping a rung, easing herself up. The man waits, and offers her the hand which isn't holding a cigarette. "Peter," he beams.

"Joy," she offers in return. Now that she's up here, the music is a physical force, thrumming through thick walls and empty windows. He leads her into the room, still smoking, and she has the impression of chintzy furniture tortured by birds and rainwater, spider webs layered thickly over the ceiling.

Peter hands her a beer, slamming the bottle open against a table edge. She accepts it carefully, wiping the rim before putting her lips to it. "You like this?" he says loudly, his hair gleaming like copper in the hazy light, and she nods. He smiles like a wolf.

There are about forty bodies in the space, mostly older than she'd have expected – some even in their thirties. They are dancing in a listless, bobbing sort of way. The music is some kind of European house, not all that different to a normal nightclub anywhere. Perhaps the location is the only subversive thing about this gathering.

Peter is waving at a girl, who walks over to them. "My twin sister, Sigrid," he says into Joy's ear. She has the same shade of hair, matte and unruly. Joy smiles uncertainly and she responds by leaning forward for a kiss, which ends awkwardly as she moves back while Joy is leaning in for the other cheek. "Not very rock and roll," says Sigrid cheerfully, and drags them both onto the dance floor. It's been a while since Joy has done this. She stands swaying for a while before falling into the rhythm, though she is stiff next to long-limbed, dexterous Peter and Sigrid.

After twelve songs or so, Joy begins to feel bored, and this too is something she remembers from her clubbing days. Even when the melodies vary, all dancing seems to be against the same beat. These tunes, all cool detached top notes with electronic riffs, feel assembled from parts by a robot.

Around the third time she has this thought, her beer dangling emptily, Peter nods at the window and Sigrid smiles, then all three of them are scampering down the ladder like children into the damp night air. "Enough," says Sigrid, as if instructing an apprentice. "The art of parties is knowing when to leave."

"Who organises this?" says Joy, eliciting another shrug from Peter. "Someone. Some people. They come here from the town. There is not much happening here on Rügen, I think. They party and they leave. We heard about this from a friend."

"Where in Germany do you come from?"

"Where in Germany?" Peter mimics. "Stockholm. Did you think I sound German?"

Joy is about to apologise when they laugh and instead she asks, "How long have you been here?"

"On the island?" Peter shrugs. "Yesterday. It's easy to get here, Sweden is just –" He gestures vaguely towards the trees, to the dappled water beyond. They reach a sandy, shallow slope, dotted with fir trees sweeping down to the unseen ocean. It is tempting to suggest a dip in the dark, but they were warned at the youth hostel about dangerous currents, and the water is probably cold. Already, the evening is falling into more orderly lines, and Joy instinctively knows the single aberration of the not-quite-rave is all she has appetite for. She is aware of her sensible shoes, her glasses, her utter lack of what Sigrid would call "rock and roll". But that is fine. She will sit for a time with her new friends, then head to bed.

"You are staying nearby?"

"In the Jugendherberge." She gargles her 'r's a little to sound like a more proficient speaker.

"Oh." Sigrid wrinkles her nose. "We passed by earlier. All neat, ping pong table and barbecue pit outside? I don 't know why people stay."

"But a party is okay?"

"That is different. The building is empty, ruined, we don't pretend it's fine, we see it and we dance. But that side – painted white, pretending it's so nice and perfect, no."

Joy takes a pull from her beer, not sure she can formulate a coherent response.

"Do you know the history of this?" says Peter.

"Of course. We 're here to experience the place."

"My grandmother wanted to stay here," says Sigrid unexpectedly. "I read her old diaries, when she died. She talked about Prora like paradise. How great the Führer was, to build this. Cheap holidays for workers."

"Kraft durch Freude," says Joy.

"Freedom through happiness, yes. You have researched."

"Your grandmother?"

"She was German. So were my parents."

"And now you're here instead of her."

"We thought we would see if there is any furniture left in the bedrooms," says Peter. "But now I think we will sleep here. Siggy? Here it is nice."

"If no rain." Sigrid rests her head on Peter's bony knee, her hair fanning over his lap. He leans forward, his skinny back arching, and kisses her hard on the mouth. She rises on her elbows. When they are done, Peter winks at Joy. "She is not really my twin."

"Did you say that?" Sigrid tilts her head back. "He does that sometimes. It is maybe amusing because we look similar."

"You believed?" Peter waggles his ring finger at her. "Wife, not sister."

"Congratulations," is all Joy can think to say.

"See how it turns out before you congratulate."

Sigrid smacks him across the shoulder. "Joy, where are you from?"

"Hackney. East London."

"I do not know it. Do you have something like this?"

"A five-kilometre concrete hotel built by the Nazi Labour Front? No."

"Then no wonder you come here to see it."

Joy checks her phone. No messages or missed calls – everything must be all right. She is surprised by the time, later than she thought. The students will be asleep by now, or at least in bed. They have an early start in the morning, a visit to the museum and then a guided tour of those parts of the ruins it is safe to walk in. The ballroom, the many swimming pools, the dining hall designed to serve meals for twenty thousand in shifts. A sandwich lunch, provided by the youth hostel, then back on the coach for more history.

This is meant to be the exciting part of her job, but so far it has been largely pedestrian. The only requirement is they return with the same number of students they left with. This evening – she has a flash of how odd it is, like a movie, to be here. The Swedes are completely relaxed, as if used to the loose ebb and flow of people. They enjoy her company – they must do, or they wouldn't still be here – but at the end of the evening they will not be swapping e-mail addresses or promising to add each other on Facebook.

"Where will you go after this?" says Peter, combing Sigrid's long hair with his fingers.

"We'll head along the coast for a bit – to see the towers, the watchtowers – "

"Grenzturm."

"Is that them? The ones they used to look out for people trying to escape."

"Yes, Grenzturm. For anyone swimming to the West. Searchlights level with the water to spot them more easily. Still people tried, and got shot. My aunt froze to death. She thought it would be easier in the winter."

Sigrid volunteers this so matter-of-factly that Joy takes a moment to be sure she has heard it. "Your family was here?"

"My aunt married someone from here. My mother was in Berlin."

"Which side?"

"East, of course. We were all East. She could see the wall from her bedroom window, when she was a girl. So close. There was one viewing platform on the other side. People from the West stood there, waving or just looking, with signboards like 'Down with Communism' or 'We are solidarity with you'. My mother waved

137

back sometimes. Then one day, she was looking, and you know, she saw – "

"She saw herself, a doppelganger in the West," says Peter in a ghost-story voice.

Sigrid smacks him. "No. You are a dick. She saw Beata, her best friend from school."

"How did she get across?"

"She didn't know. People crossed, and of course you wouldn't tell your friends before you went. Beata waved, but maybe not at her. She never saw her again. Later, they came and covered all the windows with bricks."

"We're going to Berlin, with the students. Leipzig, then Berlin."

"Bernauerstrasse, my mother's street. You should visit. There is still a platform there, and they have kept a part of the wall. For souvenir."

"Did she ever get out?"

"No, she didn't try." Sigrid's beautiful face is unreadable. Peter has tuned out, not unsympathetically, but Joy can tell he has heard this story more than once. "We left like everyone else, when the wall fell."

"1990," says Joy automatically, less like a teacher than a schoolgirl at a quiz, hand in the air.

"It's funny, we heard it was happening, but my mother had a cold so she slept early that night. My father didn't care about the news, he said nothing would ever change, just one wall won't make a difference. But the next day our neighbour said what are you doing, you are missing the biggest event of your life. So we drove there, not very far, then there were so many people we couldn't move. We got out and walked. There was a big smash in the concrete, nothing like we've ever seen, all the way through the two walls, outer and in. We went through and the people on the other side were like us, but not so, what, grey? A woman put her hand on my cheek and gave me sweets."

"And you were in the West."

"For a few hours, then we went back, I had to do homework and my mother wanted to cook dinner. We went across again on the weekend. Fewer people, and more wall missing. It was more normal to walk across, and no one welcomed us like before. I asked my mother where the people with the sweets were. She laughed and said life in the West would not always be so much fun. A few weeks later we moved to Sweden."

"Why Sweden?"

"Why not? It was the West. She hadn't seen anything West. Maybe she remembered her sister, trying to swim to Sweden. Not so far, but far enough."

There is a silence, then Peter says, gently, "They came to Sweden so she could meet me." It sounds like a joke, but there is a stillness in his voice that was not there before. He lowers himself onto his elbows so Sigrid can fit her body against his, sliding together as if their curves and grooves were made to match.

"And now," says Sigrid, "I am Swedish."

"But you came back."

"I wanted to see."

"You have walls in your country too? London Wall," says Peter.

"That was gone long ago. Anyway the Romans built it to keep people out, not in."

"Most walls do both," says Sigrid.

They talk about the next day. The Swedes have no plan, they will hitchhike off Rügen, see where they end up next, or maybe take a ferry to Norway. They have a bit of money saved up, and travel is cheap in summer when you spend most nights in the open.

And behind them, still visible in the moonlight, is the great concrete slab of Prora. Really, they are between two walls, that and the screen of trees shielding them from the full force of the sea. Joy is looking forward to seeing what remains of the Berlin wall – *Mauer*, she remembers, not *Wand* like an interior wall. The few stretches they have allowed to remain, the line that marks the rest. Are there walls where she comes from? Ones around the estate, when she was growing up. To keep people out or in?

This feels like the end of the night, the wind softening its tone like a lullaby, like the last slow song before the lights come on. How unlikely, that she should be here, hundreds of miles from where she was born. She carefully brushes sand off her blouse and thinks, *I should get back*, but stays a moment longer, enjoying the sounds and sap-smells of the night.

Peter and Sigrid are quiet now, but there isn't enough light to tell if they are asleep. She doesn't want to speak, it would spoil something, whatever is circling in the air around them. The ground, cushioned by pine needles, seems to mould itself to her body.

Joy collects German compound words – enjoying how they are concertinaed together, even the term for them: *Bandwurmwörter*, tapeworm words. There is always one for the specific sensation of each moment. Right now: *Waldeinsamkeit*, the feeling of being alone in the woods. As she shuts her eyes, they slide through her mind like beads on a string. *Schadenfreude*, of course. *Verschlimmbesserung*, a so-called improvement that actually makes things worse. *Schwellenangst*, the fear of crossing thresholds or boundaries.

Joy dreams of being in a maze, of running through a limitless number of turnings and crossroads, all of which might lead to more choices, or to a dead end. On either side of her are walls too high and smooth to climb, so tall she can only dimly see the sky above her, and a glimmer of the moon. Behind the walls, she somehow knows, are all the people she has lost, but on this side just her, just the path ahead.

She wakes up with a niggle of disquiet in her mind, a persistent crick in her neck, but most of all a warmth and well-being that radiates through every cell in her body. The sun is already up, an intense point low in the swimming-pool sky. A moment of panic as she looks at her watch. Not yet seven. She has plenty of time to walk back, shower, and present herself at breakfast, respectable Miss Hammond once again, as if none of this has happened.

The Swedes are still asleep beside her, their skin even paler against the tangle of red hair by daylight. She looks at them a moment, decides against taking a picture, and waves goodbye although they cannot see her.

It is not far to the hostel, and she allows herself to meander through the trees. Prora is to her right. She looks hard but cannot work out which set of windows the party was in. Even with the graffiti as a marker, the surface is too uniform. To her left is the Baltic Sea, flexing its surface with strong, regular waves. The green-black water reaches all the way to the horizon, but she imagines that she can just see, in the distance, other lands.

Job

Barry McKinley

Diary - London - 11 April 1979

I have no idea what I'm doing in this drawing office. I am surrounded by skilled architects, structural engineers and designers. I am an island of incompetence in an ocean of technical talent, one step up from a secretary and ten steps down from everybody else.

Dave Rennie stands at the desk beside me. He is a twenty-two-year-old Londoner with a mass of raw experience, gained from working on the designs for chemical plants and North Sea oil platforms. A little while ago he leaned across the gap between desks and asked, with genuine curiosity, "How did you ever get this job?"

"Simple," I explained, "the man who hired me is trying to fuck me."

Dave Rennie laughed, but a pain shot through his heart. He is not a handsome young man like yours truly and consequently has no option but to rely on his ability.

And, as everybody knows, ability fades.

Two months ago I came to this office on Mitcham Road for an interview with the project manager. Mr. Longley wore a loose wedding ring that slid back and forth on his finger like a bead on an abacus. When he reclined in his swivel chair his neck disappeared into the striped material that was part shirt, part optical illusion. He looked up from his notes and was clearly surprised by my youth.

"Oh!" He said; his eyes dragging over my body like a stoker's rake. "You're quite ... splendid. Please do sit down."

I found my attention drifting towards a framed photo on his desk; it showed a debonair and rascally gent with a spotted tie, trimmed moustache and a large toss of wavy hair. I wondered if it was his father, or perhaps a lesser known villain from Edwardian vaudeville.

Did I mention I was stoned?

"So, Jack," he said, "you have worked in the nuclear power industry before?"

"Yes," I replied, "I worked for a French uranium company, back in Ireland. Exploration, that sort of thing."

"Parlez-vous Francais?" he asked.

"Oui," I responded nonchalantly, "un petit peu."

He was impressed, but what he didn't know was that he had just witnessed the usage of my entire French vocabulary.

"You are familiar with Calder Hall?"

"Calder Hall," I replied, "yes, of course. In my mind I saw a great, stately pile occupied by Mr. Toad; a nearby lake with Ratty and Mole in a rowing boat."

I was incredibly stoned.

"We need somebody to oversee the decontamination systems at Calder Hall. Also there is a cladding maintenance issue, straightforward stuff, five millimetre stainless steel. You've worked with that?"

"Absolutely," I replied, my teeth parting slightly to allow the giant lies to escape.

Then he moved off in a completely unpredicted direction. "I've never been to Ireland," he said, "a lot of British people are put off. The political thing, you know. Things are difficult."

I agreed. Things were difficult.

"You don't have any ..."

He was too polite to finish the question, but I shook my head anyway, assuming he was referring to evil political affiliations.

"No, no," I said, putting on a west Brit accent, "I'm from the republic", as if that explained anything.

"Yes, yes," he nodded with a combination of embarrassment and complete geographical confusion. "You're miles away."

"Miles," I echoed.

He decided to return to a more comfortable topic. "I should give you a little info about the company. What you see on this level is a little less than a third of our operations. We're spread over four floors in the building. Upstairs, engineering; downstairs, civil. We're the technical boffins. You're the second new man; Raymond over there joined us about four weeks ago. Wife left him. Messy, messy, messy business. You are not married, are you?"

"No," I said.

"I expect you have a girlfriend?"

"No," I said, thinking of all the young women, drawn by my looks but repulsed by my personality, "I'm as free as the day I was born."

The temperature rose slightly in the cubicle. He stubbed out his half-smoked Rothmans and lit another. We had a moment of silence as he searched for words to cover his desire.

"We'll soon be changing the project name," he said, "but it's just a PR exercise. Around here we'll continue to call it Windscale."

A mushroom cloud parted inside my head. The recruitment agency had said very little about the job. They simply referred to it as a prestigious life-changing opportunity. They entirely forgot to mention the giant outlet pipe that crapped, like Godzilla's ass, great radioactive turds into the Irish Sea.

"Sellafield will be the new name."

"Sellafield," I said, nodding my approval. Sell-A-Field. It sounded so harmless, like something a farmer might do if he were strapped for cash.

Mr. Longley continued to talk, but my mind was somewhere else. I had a mental image of a giant atomic shock wave blasting across the ocean, picking up trawlers and ferries, flinging saltwater and mackerel into the heart of the Irish midlands. I pictured drowned cats and floating coffins, pulled from the soil like loose fencing pickets. I watched partially fried dogs yelping on half-submerged rooftops while men and women, as ragged as their migrant forbears, crawled with exhaustion on islands of bobbing debris. I saw a perfect globe of brilliant light, flashing like hot magnesium, eating up all the colours in the world, swallowing everything, even shadow.

Only a moral dwarf would even consider accepting a job like this. And I was that dwarf.

"What's the salary?" I asked brightly.

"Starting at eleven thousand a year, and please call me Chris."

A cluster of amphetamine crystals dissolved inside my head like temporal lobe popcorn. My eyes opened wide and sparkled and a grin flashed on like a spotlight. Mr. Longley took this behaviour as a small flirtation. He lost his way with words and grasped at the first notion that drifted into reach.

"I g-g-go to the theatre, sometimes," he stuttered, "the West End. It's rather fabulous."

This harmless statement actually came to my ears, deciphered and translated: "Are you interested in sodomy?" it said.

I said yes, yes, I was. I liked it very much. I admitted that I grew up in a small town and we didn't have a whole lot of it – Theatre, I couldn't be sure about the sodomy.

"There's nothing quite as wonderful as live theatre," he said.

I nodded with enthusiasm, keeping a lid on the opinion that theatre is nothing but fat people in wigs with loud voices.

Or is that opera?

"We must go sometime ..." he said, "together."

"Oh yes," I replied, "we must."

Meanwhile, the amphetamine pixies pulled back the skin on my cheeks and gave me an expression of deranged curiosity. I imagined I looked like a barracuda in a wind tunnel. Chris Longley found himself matching my intensity of speech. He asked me a flurry of questions about my home life in Ireland. Was I enjoying London? How long had I been here? I told him only a week and he trilled. "A w-w-eek, Oh my goodness, you are seeing everything through such new eyes, n-n-new eyes." He stared into my new blue eyes and transmitted a bright red laser of lust. "Still, I'm sure you were upset leaving h-h-home."

I left h-h-home on a Sunday night. The railway station was clotted with Sparrow Mammies, the tiny women who peck at their children, mostly girls in striped UCD scarves. The daughters try to look sophisticated while the Sparrow Mammies pinch their arms for good luck, and then hand them those small packs of disposable paper tissues for the perpetual winter snuffling.

Smoke and jostling filled the carriages. Three men in crumpled suits, who looked like they had spent a losing day at the races, sat opposite me drinking small bottles of Guinness. A folded newspaper rested on the table between them, a crossword barely started, and abandoned. People coughed for fear that silence might take hold.

Athy, Kildare, Newbridge.

We picked up speed, and then stopped just as suddenly. Doors opened and slammed shut as more excited students climbed aboard, heading for their cold water bedsits with the barred basement windows, mildew-speckled ceilings and the bathtubs discoloured with oxidised swirls. The poverty of rural Ireland accelerated and swept past the windows in a dun-coloured diorama of depressing decay, pock-marked with abandoned rusty tractors and unpainted houses where men in dirty shirts plotted suicide by hanging from a rafter. They don't call them Bun-gallows for nothing.

No. I did not feel sadness for all that I left behind.

"I have to ask you about secrets." Chris Longley said, regaining his breath and composure; his hushed words trailed off and vanished mysteriously in the air.

"Secrets?" I replied, wondering if he was about to quiz me on my dismal academic results or the bank loan that was never repaid. Prompted by my blank expression, he slid a printed sheet of paper across the desk.

"Official Secrets," he said.

The page was densely written and repeatedly photocopied until the words bled together like melted wax. The large print at the top of the page referred to the "1920 Act." Chris Longley unscrewed a fountain pen and I signed without trying to decipher the molten gibberish.

"I think you will be happy here," he said.

I put my free hand on top of his and said yes, I thought I would be very happy.

He pointed to the dapper gent in the photograph. "Tom Tuohy," he explained, "your fellow countryman, well, he was born in the UK to Irish parents; a personal hero of mine."

He went on to tell me *The Tale of Tom Tuohy* in all its fabulous detail, a story so outrageous that only a crazy Paddy could be at its centre.

During the great Windscale fire of 1957, when it looked like the whole place was going up in smoke, Site Manager Tuohy was the man who saved the day. He pulled on his protective gear, climbed the burning reactor and peered into its very heart. He listened to its breath as it sucked in air from every corridor. He patted its heaving hungry belly and then made the decision to shut off the cooling fans and pump in thousands of gallons of water.

"Outrageous," Chris Longley exclaimed, "this was eleven tons of uranium, burning at over a thousand degrees Celsius. The concrete shielding was withering under the extreme heat. As you know, molten metal causes water to oxidise. Hydrogen, explosive hydrogen, expanding into every nook of the cauldron! Tom Tuohy ordered the evacuation of the building, but for himself and the fire chief. He turned on the hoses and miraculously the inferno was extinguished."

Chris Longley took out a handkerchief and dabbed his cheeks which were now quite rosy, giving the impression that he too had been standing close to flame. He was breathless as he asked me, straight up, if I thought I could fill Tom Tuohy's large, radioactive shoes and I said "Yes sir," without the slightest hesitation.

He looked into my core, past the smouldering amphetamine fire, through the pressurised cloud of unshakable confidence and into the fast-breeding madness of a 20-year-old who was ready, willing and able to light a fuse and burn up the world. We shook hands. I turned and left Chris Longley's office, knowing that his eyes were all over me, but I didn't care. I now had something special, something beyond all credibility. I had something that half of Ireland would kill for.

I had a job.

Doted

Jenn Ashworth

Doted is a strange word, isn't it? On the one hand it means a fondness or an uncritical affection; the feeling an adult might have for a small child or a pet dog. A couple newly in love might dote on each other too. When our hypothetical couple get to know each other better, this doting wears off because the honeymoon stage is just a stage and once it passes there's a tendency for the cold light of day to get into things. The relationship is never the same again: scientists on the internet say you get two years: tops. That first doting is immaturity and foolishness. A kind of infirmity; a lack of sound judgment: caused by love. The word is related to *dotage*; an archaic expression denoting madness, senility, dementia. When Lear curses Goneril, first with sterility and then, if she must have a child, with an ungrateful one, she dismisses his ranting as merely a product of his dotage. Her father's cursing doesn't count because he's too fond and too old.

When I was little I was close to Mum's parents, and never met Dad's. It came as a surprise to me that they were dead. When I found out, I asked him when and how his Mum went. I'd never known anyone who had died before.

"It happened some time previously and from a lack of breath," he said. Then he slapped at his leg and forced out a laugh. It was long and loud; a machine gun rattle.

When I was really little, I used to join in the laughing. He had a reputation, amongst people who didn't know him, for being a good fun kind of guy. Life and soul. Something like that. When I was a little older, I noticed something. This laugh, be it ever so loud and out of control, was something he performed with his eyes open. He kept his eye on you because he wanted to make sure, perhaps, that you got the joke. That there would be no more questions. He fed himself his own punch-lines too, well-prepared and wedged into the conversation whether they made sense, or not.

"Did you go to her funeral? Where was it? In a church?"

I'm like a dog with a bone sometimes. That's what people say about me. I didn't drop it. I never do.

"The only thing you need to know is this," he said, "the good Lord said come forth but she came fifth, and only won a bag of nuts," he bent over laughing, yelping with it. It sounded hard. Like work, like pain.

I asked him what his favourite subject at school was.

"Noughts and crosses," he said, then the laugh. This time, it sounded more like what it was: pleasure at my frustration.

I asked which colour was his favourite.

"What's yours?" he said.

"Red."

"Yes, that's mine as well."

I wouldn't hold his hand. Even then I knew that laugh was too loud, too long. He wasn't in complete control over it. Other people walking through town that afternoon turned their heads to look at us. He became shameful.

Despite the laughing Dad never seemed that happy. He worked twelve hour shifts in a factory that turned plain cardboard into waxed cardboard and turned the waxed cardboard into fish finger boxes (I only know this because Grandad worked there too). Dad complained about the long hours and having to come home to an untidy house full of children that were rapidly outgrowing it. His primary pleasure in life was walking the dogs. There were two: a black and tan mongrel beset with persistent, incurable mange that Dad had adopted from the RSPCA and called Max, after Mad Max, because as soon as he'd brought the puppy into the house, the thing had gone totally crazy and started to play the fool, jumping into the air and snapping at flies buzzing around the lampshades. That dog had grown up into whatever the canine equivalent of a depressive recluse is and when it wasn't being walked, slept under Mum and Dad's bed. We could hear it scratching itself raw, spraying dandruff over the carpet and whimpering through the artex-swirled ceiling.

After we got Max, Dad developed an interest in wildfowling, guns and the shooting of birds. He decided he needed another dog, a better one than Max. So Earl arrived: an expensive, pedigree Black Labrador that lived outside in a large kennel Dad built out of old wooden pallets from the paper factory especially for him. Earl was not a pet, and not to be petted. We weren't to feel sorry for him, out in the cold on his own. Earl was a working gun-dog and the twice daily walks which were mere exercise for Max and a time to do his business were training periods for Earl. Dad took them seriously and conducted the sessions for an audience of plastic, life-sized decoys of teal and mallard. He directed the action with a stop-watch and a stick. For a time, not a long time, I got up early, before school, and accompanied Dad, Mad Max and Earl on these walks/training sessions.

We lived in a small terraced house – a two up, two down that had been, sometime in the Seventies, been made into a three up, two down. The place lay in a warren of terraced houses just like it, between the town centre and one of the arterial roads out of Preston to the south. Grey though it was, we were only fifteen minutes' walk away from the nature reserves and farmland on the south bank of the Ribble and the dirty footpath alongside the north bank of the river which led along it to the docks.

The mornings I went out with Dad he strode too fast for me and I had to trot alongside him to catch up. He had a routine and the dogs knew it. Off the leads here, stop to collect sticks here, pause to look at the river and check the weather here, perhaps a cigarette and a chance to do your business here, turn and come back here. I was additional, an imposition. He mainly ignored me, walking fast and, as he walked, gesticulating and muttering under his breath. Sometimes he would lose himself completely and start speaking out loud. It never made much sense, but the odd phrase or two became clear: *picking his teeth up off the floor and time and time and time again and have it out once and for all and no need to get so aerated and told you, more than once, to stop creating*. He'd get all worked up and walk faster and faster, jabbing his finger in mid-air, droplets of spit flying off his lips and building up at the corners of his mouth.

What was he doing? Replaying, perhaps, a scene of injustice he'd suffered at the paper factory, or allowing himself the chance to say something to a superior he'd never be able to get away with in real life. Maybe he was talking to his Mum, getting off his chest things he should have made time to say before she'd had her lack of breath and been called forth. He could have been hearing voices: paranoid, nasty little accusations about his wife, his eldest daughter, about how people always seemed to be staring at him, judging him, wanting something, maybe planning to steal or kill something that belonged to him. Why would they do that? The bastard, ungrateful kids. Or the clever fucks writing newspaper articles. Smart Alecks on the telly, every night, without fail.

It frightened me. I wanted him to stop doing it. His rages, tantrums, his smashings up of things and people were evidence enough that there was something not quite right. Worse after drink, but not much better without it. But this muttering to an invisible audience was worse, somehow. It was public and embarrassing. I asked him about it. Of course I did.

"What are you talking about?"

He'd frown, wave me away, tell me to shut up. Sometimes, I would insist.

"You're *arguing* with yourself. What are you thinking?"

My demanding infuriated him, however I worded the question, smartest of all Smart Alecks, a little bastard fully determined not to be frustrated this time, he waved me away or ignored me entirely. He would carry on ranting or he would explode and drag me back to the house by my shoulder, my arm, my hair, throwing me through the front door and complaining to Mum that, *yet again*, I'd managed to *ruin everything* and would she do something with me, *once and for all*, otherwise he *wasn't going to be responsible* for the harm he would do to himself or someone closer. When I was with him he was beside himself.

Alone with Mum and complaining about him, she'd only sigh wearily.

"What did you say to him this time? You must have said something to set him off," she'd ask.

"Nothing," I'd reply. "I said nothing."

I go to the best uni that will take me and study English Literature because he can barely read and it will piss him off. But all reading *King Lear* does is make me want to call Mum. I stand at a payphone and we skirt around what I want to ask, giving it plenty of room to breathe; to come forth.

She says, *of course you were his firstborn, and when you came along, up until you were two years old, he doted on you.*

Doted is the actual word Mum uses when she tells me about this, the word she uses to batter back the memories I have. So I will give you only three examples because then you will know I am not lying and because all fairy tales obey the Rule of Three.

One
This man who doted on me until I was two deliberately slammed the front door on my hand. Then he did it again. My sister called 999 and told the operator he was killing me. When the police arrived he spoke to them in the kitchen and denied everything. Later, when invited again to answer questions, he told a social worker that I'd been "creating" and he'd been trying to pull me into the house, to close the door and stop me from running away.

Two
This man who doted on me until I was two was cleaning his shotgun in the living room when something I said or did angered him and he held it against my head and told my brother and sister to watch. Told them about leprosy. I thought that was what Lazarus had died of but I wasn't sure. I knew better than to ask: he didn't read the Bible. He told them it was very catching and they had to treat me as if I had it from this day forward. He hit me on the forehead with the end of the gun. Pushed me over with it. Told me if I ran out of the house and got run over he would stamp on my dead body and laugh.

Three
I am ten years old, in pain, irritable. We are all at the kitchen table, eating. My mother has just taken me into the bathroom and run the shower on full blast and told me that I'm not ill: this is a good thing. I can have a baby now.

I am wet between the legs and I get up to fetch my water glass from the living room. When I forget to close the kitchen door, this man who doted on me until I was two takes my plate off the table and throws it into the sink, where it smashes spectacularly, gravy hitting the window.

My sister smiles slyly.

Mum asks him to show some patience.

He says: *I showed enough patience when she first started; the dirty little bitch. She can't use it as an excuse all week.*

After Dad threw us out we visited my Uncle Jackie and borrowed clothes from my cousins to tide us over. A bit later, Granddad and Jackie visited Dad at the house. Apparently they held Dad down on the couch while he thrashed and ranted and foamed, just to give Mum a chance to duck in and grab our things. She'd let us know there wouldn't be time to collect everything. The three of us – me, my sister and brother – made lists. We weren't to expect to get everything from the list. I asked for Toby Bear, a bashed metal colander and my Steven Livingstone adventure game books with the lime green spines, which, I argued, were numbered and came as a set and so counted as only one item. For herself, Mum took a pair of peacock feather pattered curtains she wanted for making into a quilt, a dressing table set made of irradiated green glass and a banana box she'd covered with brown paper and thumb tacks to look like a treasure chest. Inside were the family photographs.

I learned about the rule of three that winter from my English teacher. There are three Billy Goats Gruff. Rumplestiltskin visits three times. How many ugly sisters does Cinderella have? Our Cordelia had two. Three adjectives were very much excellently better than two. Two examples of a thing allows us to detect a pattern, and, when the third breaks it, we'll feel both relieved and surprised. It will be, Mrs Butterworth promised, satisfying. We'd be marked on our creative use of the technique. Blood, sweat, tears.

Mum lies on the couch under her peacock tail curtains and sifts through her treasure box, touching our paper baby faces.

One

In this photograph I am nine months old and improbably blonde. Wearing a silver christening bracelet. On a swing, laughing. The sun is bright: I'm wearing some pale, striped cotton thing. There's a tall privet hedge behind me and the depth of field renders my skin breath-takingly perfect; the hedge is a whirl of dense green against a late-spring sky a shade of blue that belongs to the eighties: you just don't get it anymore. Dad isn't in the picture because he is lying on the grass under the swing tickling my feet to make me laugh. The swing-park is a park-and-ride now.

Two
I am a toddler, perhaps eighteen months old. Wearing a duffel coat and sitting in a ride on Blackpool Pleasure beach. The ride consists of a seat (into which I am strapped) attached to a red and yellow plastic disc that rotates, flashes lights and plays *It's a Small World After All*. At the height of the disc's rotation I am four feet off the ground, in arm's reach of Dad who is in the photograph, holding my hand and smiling.

Three
I am two now and I am wearing a pink dress and white Clark's shoes and white ankle socks with a frill around the top of them. The dress has a yellow kite and a blue balloon appliquéd onto it. Dad is holding me up. He is wearing a vest and brown corduroy flares. He is standing in front of a blue mini car on the street in front of our house. I am frowning and pointing at the camera. *Go away.* He is doing the laugh: I can tell by how he's holding his shoulders; the way his tongue is raised out of his mouth.

I am still on the phone to Mum. I am always on the phone to Mum.
"When did he stop doting on me?" I ask.
Except I don't use these words. I can't bear to say them out loud. I say something like, "What changed?" or perhaps I do the laugh I have learned and say, "Well that's not quite how I remember it."
The receiver is slippery in my hand.
"You learned to talk," she says, matter of factly. As if it's obvious. Family common knowledge. "You started talking, and asking questions, and you wouldn't stop."

Mad Max died before I went to university. He went quickly, during the night. It was probably a heart attack caused by old age and neglect. Can a dog die of mange? Earl went a couple of years later. Dad telephoned me to tell me what had happened when I was in a pub in Sheffield, having lunch with a friend. Hadn't spoken to my father in months. I tried to make my excuses but he talked over me, ploughed on, insisted I listen while he told me what the vet had told him.

Earl still slept outside, and Dad had been woken in the night by the sound of his metal water bowl overturning and scraping against the paving slab as the dog thrashed and yelped, its mouth foaming. He'd carried him in his arms – a 50 pound baby – into the back of his car and turned up at the emergency clinic wearing only his vest and some old cords.

Dad went off at a tangent here. He talked about the mess on the inside of the car; the difficulty in driving with the dog having seizures beside him; the bite on his hand the vet had advised him to "get looked at". He digressed further and described what a gentle nature the dog had; about how well disciplined and loyal he was, about how this bite on the hand that had fed him wasn't evidence of anything to do with the dog's character but only how affected he'd been by whatever sudden illness he was suffering from. A brain tumour, perhaps.

What he didn't tell me but found its way into his story anyway: the dog had a crate in the back of the car and Dad was assiduous about using it but this time, for Earl's last journey, Dad had him in the front passenger seat, stroking him as he turned the steering wheel with one bloodied hand.

Too dramatic?

As he spoke, going on and on in grief-stricken circles, I made apologetic gestures towards my friend; wiped curly fries through a puddle of mayonnaise on the side of my plate; signalled for another pint. You could still smoke inside pubs then. I worked my way through my packet, smoking one after the other until my eyes were dry and my throat stung.

Dad told me about our street; how it had gone downhill since we'd moved out. Scallies and junkies and taken to hanging about in the back ginnel to do their deals. Maybe one of the scallies was worried about being caught with something on him he shouldn't have and had chucked a bit of contraband over the wall. That was the word he used: *contraband*. And guess what? The dog really did have something in its stomach, some piece of latex, which implied it might have eaten something it shouldn't. Perhaps cocaine or amphetamine, the vet had suggested, judging by the symptoms of its death. The vet was very curious about it all. Was going to do a post-mortem. Maybe even get the police involved. She'd know for sure in a day or so. She was a woman but she was still very good.

Very sympathetic, but women are, aren't they? I said nothing.

Dad started from the beginning. He wanted to tell me the story again right back from the time he was awoken in the dead of night by the metallic noise of the water-bowl being tipped over and hitting the flags in the yard.

"I'm out, Dad. I can't talk anymore. I'm with a friend. I'll ring you back tomorrow, yeah? Let me know what the vet says."

I didn't phone him back, even though Mum, who had been divorced from him for seven years, said she was worried about him, that she felt sorry for him.

The new dog is another black Labrador and its name is Princess. I haven't spoken to Dad in several years now and I doubt, very much, that I will again. But I still live where I used to and so does he. Very often, as I am driving my children around I see him crossing that main arterial road on the way to the river, wearing camouflage gear with a lead in his hands. I had to stop at two kids. Medical reasons. I have one he barely knows and probably wouldn't recognise and another he has never met. He's opened savings accounts and divided my inheritance between the two of them all the same. Whenever I see him, Princess is trotting fast, trying hard to keep up, and Dad is shouting as he walks. He is gesturing to himself. He jabs the innocent air with such force that people have to cross the street to avoid him. Sometimes I want to stop the car and ask him a question but I always drive on and leave him to it.

My father dotes. When a tree's heartwood rots, botanists describe the trunk as *doted* so perhaps I dote too. It is eminently possible, given the realities of Elizabethan theatrical practice, that for some early productions of *King Lear*, Cordelia and the fool were double cast. "*My poor fool is hanged*", Lear says, and the audience in the know, the audience who have, just for the moment, suspended their suspension of disbelief and allowed themselves to notice that the actor playing Cordelia is also playing the fool, is allowed the tiniest of morbid chuckles. They're allowed to pat themselves on the back: they weren't fooled after all; they always knew Cordelia was an idiot in disguise, and a poor one at that.

About the Authors

CHLOE ARIDJIS grew up in the Netherlands and Mexico City and has a doctorate from Oxford in nineteenth-century French poetry and magic shows. Her debut novel *Book of Clouds* was awarded the French Prix du Premier Roman Etranger. She is a 2014 recipient of the Guggenheim Fellowship.

JENN ASHWORTH's first novel, *A Kind of Intimacy*, was published in 2009 and won a Betty Trask Award. On the publication of her second, *Cold Light* (Sceptre, 2011) she was featured on the BBC's The Culture Show as one of the UK's twelve best new writers. Her third novel *The Friday Gospels* (2013) is published by Sceptre. She lives in Lancashire and teaches Creative Writing at Lancaster University.

SEAN BEAUDOIN is the author of five novels, including the old school noir mystery *You Killed Wesley Payne*, the rude zombie opus *The Infects*, and the raw-throated punk band diary *Wise Young Fool*. His stories and articles have appeared in numerous publications, including the Onion, Salon, Glimmer Train, the San Francisco Chronicle, and Spirit – the inflight magazine of Southwest Airlines. He is also a founding editor of the arts and culture website TheWeeklings.com, which is hands-down the best site on the internet.

TARA ISABELLA BURTON's essays and travel writing can be found at National Geographic Traveler, Al Jazeera America, The BBC, The Atlantic, The Paris Review Daily, Los Angeles Review of Books, Salon, The New Statesman, Tin House Open Bar, The American Reader, and more. Her fiction has appeared or is forthcoming in Arc, Shimmer, PANK, and more. She is the winner of The Spectator's 2012 Shiva Naipaul Memorial Prize for travel writing. She has recently completed her first novel.

REECE CHOULES graduated in 2012 with a Creative Writing BA from LSBU. He contributes regularly to The Culture Trip with articles on film, literature and music. His short stories have appeared in The Southbank Review, Inkapature, Litro, The Dying Goose and Cigale. He was also longlisted for the 2013 Fish Publishing Short Story Competition, as well as being a finalist in the Aesthetica Short story competition and appearing in the Aesthetica Creative Writing Annual 2014. He has recently been accepted to study for an MA in Creative and Life Writing at Goldsmiths University and is working on his first novel. @ReeceChoules

SETH CLABOUGH is a professor, scholar, poet, short story writer, and novelist. He has a BA from Randolph-Macon College, an MA in English from USC, and a PhD from Aberystwyth University. David Forrer of Inkwell Management in New York represents his forthcoming debut novel and his recent writing has appeared in Poiesis Review, Fjord's Review, Citron Review, Aesthetica: the Arts & Culture Magazine, Magma Poetry, The Chaffey Review, Writer's in Education, Sixers Review, New Writing: The International Journal for the Practice and Theory of Creative Writing, Women's Studies, story South and elsewhere.

HOWARD CUNNELL is the author of the novels *Marine Boy* (2008), and *The Sea on Fire* (2012). He is the editor of Jack Kerouac's *On the Road – The Original Scroll* (2007). His next book will be a memoir: *Hard to Love*.

ANTHONY DOERR's most recent book is the novel *All the Light We Cannot See*. In 2007, he was named one of Granta's Best Young American Novelists.

CHARLIE HILL is a writer from Birmingham. He has written two novels: a political love story called *The Space Between Things*, which was described by the Observer as 'inventive and full of promise' and by the Times as 'wonderfully observed;' and a comedy of ideas called *Books*, which was heralded by both the Financial Times and the Morning Star. His short stories have appeared in a number of magazines and journals, both in print and online. Some of them are experimental, others not so ...

TRINE V. IPSEN is a Danish writer from the Southern part of the Island Zealand. She studied Creative Writing at Stirling University, Scotland, Griffith University in Australia and the University of Copenhagen in Denmark, where she is soon to start her Masters thesis on 'The Academic Merits of Creative Writing in the English Speaking World'. Her stories have been shortlisted for the Save As writing competition and a short story competition for Chilling Tales for Dark Nights. In 2015, her short story 'Else Marie' will be published in Griffith University's yearly anthology, Talent Implied.

ALEXANDER KNIGHTS is a border boy from East Anglia who now writes stories from his patch in Peckham Rye. A graduate of Birkbeck's Creative Writing MA, he works in digital publishing, has published stories in The Mechanics' Institute Review 9 and Riptide, and was recently long-listed for the Bath Short Story Award. He's interested in tech as the new fantastic. @knightswrites

POLIS LOIZOU grew up in a Cyprus of gang vendettas, money-laundering priests and bombs in strip-joints. He's now part of The Off-Off-Off-Broadway Company, a fringe theatre troupe through which he can exorcise those demons. He is redrafting and editing two novels at once, and has recently begun a third. That's what a recession does to you.

F.C. MALBY grew up in East Anglia and has taught English in the Czech Republic, the Philippines and London. Her debut novel, *Take Me to the Castle*, won The People's Book Awards 2013. Her short fiction has been longlisted in The New Writer Annual Prose and Poetry Prizes 2012 and is published in various online journals.

ALAN MCCORMICK is Writer in Residence at Kingston University Writing School, where he recently devised and co-ran the Hilary Mantel and Bonnie Greer story competitions. His short fiction has won several national prizes, been widely published in print, including in Litro and The Sunday Express, and regularly online at 3:AM Magazine and Nth Position. His story collection, *Dogsbodies and Scumsters*, was long-listed for the Edge Hill Prize in 2012. He also writes flash shorts known as 'Scumsters' in response to pictures by Jonny Voss. See more of their work, and a selection of Alan's short fiction, at www.dogsbodiesandscumsters.wordpress.com and www.scumsters.blogspot.co.uk.

LAURA MCKENNA, from Cork, Ireland, has a Masters in Creative Writing. Her short fiction and poetry have been widely published and won awards including the 2012 RTE Guide/Penguin short story prize and the 2011 Edmund Spenser poetry Prize. She was nominated for the 2014 Hennessy literary awards. She was invited to read at the 2014 Cork Spring Poetry Festival and Listowel Writer's Week. Laura's novel was a winner in the 2013 IWC Novel Fair competition. She was awarded a Literature Bursary by the Arts Council in 2012 and a Tyrone Guthrie Bursary in 2014.

BARRY MCKINLEY was nominated in 2010 for Best New Play, Irish Theatre Awards (for Elysium Nevada). He has written for BBC Radio 4 and RTE. He was shortlisted twice for the Hennessy Literary Award with the short stories, Hope I Die and The Unexpected Hotel. His most recent play, *The Last Crusader*, was staged in Dublin in 2013.

IAIN ROBINSON holds an MA in Creative Writing from Lancaster University and a PhD in Creative and Critical Writing from the University of East Anglia. His debut novel, *The Buyer*, was published by CoLiCo Press in 2014. He also writes literary criticism and has contributed a book chapter on Sarah Hall's *The Carhullan Army to Twenty-First Century Fiction: What Happens Now* (Palgrave, 2013) and his article on Will Self's *The Book of Dave* was published in Volume 2, Issue 1 of C21 Literature: Journal of 21st-century Writings (Gylphi, 2013). He is currently working on a second novel, *The Museum of Lost Houses*.

IAN SALES was only three when Neil Armstrong landed on the Moon, but he's spent the last few years writing about astronauts. His *Adrift on the Sea of Rains*, the first book of the Apollo Quartet, was published in 2012 and subsequently won the BSFA Award. The second book of the quartet, *The Eye With Which The Universe Beholds Itself*, and the third book, *Then Will The Great Wash Deep Above*, were published in 2013. The final book, *All That Outer Space Allows*, was published in 2014. He has appeared in several anthologies, and he reviews books for the science fiction magazine Interzone.

NIKESH SHUKLA is the author of the Costa First Novel – shortlisted *Coconut Unlimited*, an ebook about the 2011 riots, Generation Vexed (with Kieran Yates), a novella about food called *The Time Machine*, and Kabadasses for Channel 4 Comedy Lab. His most recent novel, *Meatspace*, was released in July 2014. His stories have appeared in the Book Slam anthology, The Moth and the Sunday Times online, and have been broadcast on BBC Radio 4. He was born in London and now lives in Bristol.

JEREMY TIANG's writing has appeared in the Guardian, Esquire, Ambit, Meanjin, the Istanbul Review, QLRS and Best New Singaporean Short Stories. He is also a playwright and translator. www.JeremyTiang.com

CHIKA UNIGWE is an Afro-Belgian writer of Nigerian origin. She is the author of fiction, poetry, articles and educational material. Her second novel, *On Black Sisters' Street*, was published by Jonathan Cape in 2009

JOANNA WALSH's writing has been published by Granta, Dalkey, Salt, and many others. Her collection of short stories, *Fractals*, is published by 3:AM Press. *Hotel* will be published by Bloomsbury USA in 2015. She runs the @Readwomen campaign.

LUCIE WHITEHOUSE was born in Gloucestershire and grew up near Stratford-on-Avon. She studied Classics at Oxford University and then worked in publishing. Her first novel, *The House at Midnight*, was published in 2008 and was followed by

The Bed I Made, which was selected for the Channel 4 TV Book Club Summer Read. *Before We Met,* her third and most recent novel, was chosen for the WHSmith/Richard and Judy Book Club Summer 2014. Her work has been read on Radio 4 and translated into eight languages.

KATE WILLIAMS fell in love with the eighteenth century whilst studying at the University of Oxford. She has a DPhil from the University of Oxford and is also a lecturer and TV consultant, appearing regularly on BBC and Channel 4 programmes to discuss her work. Her latest novel, *The Storms of War,* is the first of a trilogy about the De Witt family from 1914-1939, and was published in the UK by Orion Books in July 2014.

MICHELLE WRIGHT lives in a very messy house in Melbourne, Australia where she writes short stories and flash fiction. She is passionate about languages, literature, sanitation and science. She's won The Age Short Story Competition, the Writers Victoria Grace Marion Award, the Alan Marshall Award, the Orlando Prize and come second in the Bridport Prize for flash fiction and the Overland VU Prize. In 2013 she was awarded the Writers Victoria Templeberg Residential Writing Fellowship in Galle, Sri Lanka and in 2015 she'll spend two months in a secluded bushland setting as a Laughing Waters artist in residence.

SAMUEL WRIGHT has recently moved from London to the North East, where he is head of a new Sixth Form in Sunderland. He has previously been longlisted for the Sunday Times EFG Short Story Award, and has won the Tom Gallon Trust Award from the Society of Authors. Last year he brought out The Marshes in collaboration with photographer Josh Lustig and Tartaruga Press.

BENJAMIN ZEPHANIAH is probably one of the most high-profile international authors writing today, with an enormous breadth of appeal, equally popular with adults and children. Most well-known for his performance poetry with a political edge for adults and ground-breaking performance poetry for children, Benjamin has also written several urban novels for teenagers. Benjamin has

his own rap/reggae band and has appeared on Desert Island Discs.
He travels the world speaking about his books and poetry.

Lightning Source UK Ltd.
Milton Keynes UK
UKOW06f1441150515

251623UK00007B/77/P